"Well, I guess there really isn't any use in denying the sparks, is there?"

Her bright eyes searched his, an eagerness dancing there. One he wanted to act on. Damn the logic.

"Attraction is what it is. Even my scientific mind knows it's not logical—but it is tangible." He leaned forward on the table, his knee brushing hers. She stared at the point of contact, the place where electricity seemed to build, coursing through him.

"I'm not a judgy kind of person." She lifted her head, fixating now on his mouth. The warmth of her body teased him as she continued, her voice lower, as if confessing a secret. "But I've also never indulged in the one-night-stand gig."

"From the looks of the storm and the piles of snow out there, we'll be here far more than one night. If you're so inclined to...indulge."

\* \* \*

*The Double Deal* is part of the Alaskan Oil Barons series, the eight-book saga from *USA TODAY* bestselling author Catherine Mann!

Dear Reader,

Plotting the eight-book arc for the Alaskan Oil Barons has been an exciting adventure and an exploration of this powerful dynasty. Especially as it all takes place in such a snowy, rugged terrain! My grandparents lived in Alaska long ago, but I still vividly recall waiting for Granddad's shipment of canned salmon and moose steaks. (My younger sisters actually thought he was sending us a moose!)

The mystique of Alaska has been a blast to research, from the majestic snow to the northern lights. And yes, I got a special kick out of coming up with exotic food choices for the hero, Royce Miller, PhD, and the heroine, Naomi Steele, to share during those romantic nights trapped by a blizzard.

Snuggle up and happy reading.

Cheers,

CatherineMann.com

# CATHERINE MANN

---

## THE DOUBLE DEAL

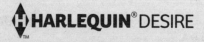
HARLEQUIN® DESIRE

Recycling programs
for this product may
not exist in your area.

ISBN-13: 978-1-335-97137-1

The Double Deal

Copyright © 2018 by Catherine Mann

**Printed in U.S.A.**

*USA TODAY* bestselling author **Catherine Mann** has won numerous awards for her novels, including both a prestigious RITA® Award and an *RT Book Reviews* Reviewers' Choice Award. After years of moving around the country bringing up four children, Catherine has settled in her home state of South Carolina, where she's active in animal rescue. For more information, visit her website, catherinemann.com.

### Books by Catherine Mann

**Harlequin Desire**

*Diamonds in the Rough*

*One Good Cowboy*
*Pursued by the Rich Rancher*
*Pregnant by the Cowboy CEO*

*The Lourdes Brothers of Key Largo*

*The Boss's Baby Arrangement*
*His Secretary's Little Secret*

*Alaskan Oil Barons*

*The Baby Claim*
*The Double Deal*

Visit her Author Profile page at Harlequin.com, or catherinemann.com, for more titles.

To my sisters, Julie and Beth

"A sister is a gift to the heart, a friend to the spirit, a golden thread to the meaning of life."
—Isadora James

# Prologue

Naomi Steele wasn't naive.

Her life had brought enough challenges to make her wise—if not jaded. She'd expected pregnancy to bring changes too. Yes, hormonal upheaval. But also miraculous transformations, full of shimmering emotions and realized dreams.

She just hadn't expected to feel such a ferocious internal roar—a primal drive—to protect her child at all costs.

Or possibly children. Plural? Twins ran in her family and having used in vitro increased her odds of fraternal twins. A wave of nerves—and nausea—hit her.

Breathe. Breathe. Focus.

With a report from the private investigator to her left and her computer screen to her right, she compared notes on the world-famous research scientist who could bring her the business coup—the security—she needed for her child. Sure, she had a large, wealthy family, and she lived in the confines of their estate outside of Anchorage, Alaska. Her suite was large. The enclosed balcony offered her magnificent views of both the bay and the mountains.

But none of that helped her feel as though she had a real stake in the family business. A legacy to share with her child. And since her pregnancy had been accomplished by in vitro fertilization with a sperm donor, she was utterly on her own to create that legacy. That lasting piece of the Steele portfolio that couldn't be taken away.

Her family was in a state of upheaval. Her father's upcoming marriage to a former business rival and the resulting merger of their two oil empires meant everyone in both families were fighting for roles in the new company—Alaska Oil Barons, Incorporated. Naomi needed to contribute to the business in a way that was undeniably hers.

And research scientist Royce Miller was her ticket to making that happen.

She let the corners of the private investigator's report brush over her thumb like a flip book, information she already knew about Royce Miller, PhD, by heart. She let her gaze fall on her computer screen, where a rare image of him filled the space. He was a brilliant man, a reclusive genius. He was all compelling eyes and brooding good looks, his intelligence as evident as his strong shoulders.

She needed him to cement her value in the family business.

Was the anonymous father of her child half that smart? Half that strong? All moot musings. She'd chosen her path as a single parent, on her own.

Up to now, that independence had suited her just fine.

Since her battle with cancer as a teenager, she'd lived her life for herself, and with abandon. She'd embraced her competitiveness. In play, and later in her work as an attorney for her family's Alaskan-based oil business. She preferred no strings in all her dealings, outside the connection to her widowed father and her siblings.

Now, she was still going her own way, but the stakes were higher than ever.

She had seen often enough how quickly a successful company could crash. And with the tumultuous merger of the Steele oil holdings with the Mikkelson oil family—thanks to her father's surprise engagement to the Mikkelson matriarch—Naomi was more concerned than ever about the future of the business. Their competitor, Johnson Oil United, was hot on their heels, hoping to use the uncertainty during the merger as a chance to surge ahead in the market.

Naomi couldn't grow complacent. She couldn't back down.

Right now, her private detective and crazy good internet skills were her best advantages in tracking down her ace in the hole.

Finding the scientist and persuading him to bring his research on ecological advancements in oil pipelines to her family was paramount. At the very least, she needed to locate him and sneak a peek at his research. Aside from the benefits to her family's company, his research could be the key to reducing environmentally based cancers, a passion she shared with her ecologist sister Delaney. Doubling the stakes, really.

After tireless searching for Dr. Miller, Naomi finally had a lead on the sequestered scientist. He'd retreated to the mountains to work on his research in an isolated but luxurious glass igloo.

Now that she'd found him, she just needed to come up with a plan to meet him. Hang out with him. And use her creative maneuvering to wrangle an afternoon together where she could work her way into his good graces and secure the deal of a lifetime.

# One

Research scientist Royce Miller didn't have a problem shifting from cerebral to alpha mode to save a woman from a hungry Alaskan grizzly that should have been hibernating.

But he needed to put on some clothes first.

Royce gathered up his jeans, boots and a parka to go over his boxers and T-shirt. Beyond the thick paned glass of his remote getaway, a shaggy brown bear stalked toward an SUV. Parked in his snow-piled driveway, the driver—someone in a blindingly pink parka—honked the horn repeatedly. The blaring would have alerted a couple of city blocks, except this happened to be the only cabin for nearly a hundred miles.

Well, not a cabin exactly.

Renting this insulated glass igloo out in the middle of nowhere had given him the irresistible opportunity to soak up some rare Alaskan rays this month as he immersed himself in developing new safety measures for oil pipelines. Not that he gave a damn about a tan, but vitamin D from sunshine was in short supply this far north and crucial for bone health, muscle mass and strength. All of which could come in handy once he stepped outdoors to say howdy to the massive grizzly closing in on the SUV holding his unexpected guest.

The "guest"? An issue he would deal with later.

Just because he valued his privacy as highly as his vintage Pascal's calculator, that didn't mean he could let the angry bear take out the dainty woman behind the wheel of the four-wheel drive. Her pink hood bobbed left and right, fast, as if she searched for options. Or help.

At least she was in a vehicle. That gave him a few precious moments to prep rather than bolt out there in the buff.

Bolting away from the glass wall, he sidestepped his Saint Bernard. "'Scuse me, Tessie."

Tessie, as in short for the scientist Nikola Tesla.

The two-year-old shaggy dog lifted her block head off her paws and tipped it to the side. She was worn-out from their time playing in the yard earlier, a long outing to stretch her legs since he'd known a blizzard was imminent. Was that why this driver had stopped here? Stranded on the way back to Anchorage? Spring was just one breath from winter up here.

His Saint Bernard narrowed her eyes, studying him intently. Sniffing the air, the dog let out a low whine, standing. Perhaps catching the scent of the bear. Not good.

"This isn't the time for curiosity, girl." Urgency pumped through him as he tugged on his jeans, pausing only to turn off his computer with a brisk click on his way by. Sensitive data secured.

From the bear and a lost tourist? Not likely.

Still, never could be too careful given the nature of his work. Patent-worthy research if all played out as he suspected. And when it came to his job, he was never wrong. The stakes were too high. Too personal.

His father had worked the old-school oil pipelines, like most of the population in the small Texas town where Royce had grown up. It had been a tight community. A loss of one sent ripples throughout that touched them all.

When his former fiancée's father had died in an explosion, Royce's world had been blown apart too. Then his fiancée miscarried their baby and left the country. Left him…

Shaking off the past, Royce dressed with methodical speed, shrugging into a fleece-lined flannel shirt, then tugging on a parka, and stepped into boots on his way to the door to deal with the massive curveball thrown at his day. This would have been the perfect secluded afternoon for productive thinking.

He'd come to the wilderness retreat for peace, a slice of time with no distractions. No question, creating a safer, ecologically friendly oil pipeline was personal.

Corporations vied to get him on their payroll, but he preferred to work solo and, thanks to selling off a few patents, he had a multimillion-dollar cushion to innovate on his own terms. Such as working here. Alone.

So much for that plan.

Thinsulate gloves were all he could afford to wear and still use the tools at his disposal to rid them of the bear's threat. A flare gun and, as a last resort, a shotgun.

"Tessie," he said firmly, "stay."

She huffed in apparent irritation at being kept inside, but she didn't budge.

"Good girl." He tossed the words of praise over his shoulder.

Bracing himself, he unlocked the door that opened into a short igloo-style tunnel. A blast of frigid air whipped inward hard and fast, damn near freezing his breath in his chest. A painful breath, as the cold air crackled in his lungs. Steeling himself, he pressed into the howl of the blizzard wind, the blaring horn roaring almost louder than the bear.

Royce pushed forward into the full slam of storm winds. If he could steer the bear away before it reached the driver, or distract the bear long enough for the woman to bolt inside...

The grizzly ambled faster toward the SUV idling

beside Royce's dual cab truck. Now that he was outside, he could see the SUV spewing sludge from the back wheels as the vehicle worked—in vain—to reverse out.

With a flying leap and roar, the beast pounded on the hood of the woman's vehicle, enormous paws taking swipes at the windshield. Even through the thick swirls of snow mixed with sleet, Royce could see the glint of long, lethal bear claws.

The time for finesse had ended.

Royce shouted, "Hey, you, teddy bear, check me out."

His voice got lost amid the car horn blending with the unforgiving blizzard. The grizzly's ears twitched but still he—or she—continued to rock the SUV, chunks of slush clotting in the shaggy coat. The blizzard dumped its fury faster and faster from the sky, wind carrying the flakes sideways in stinging icy bullets. Royce raised the flare gun and popped a flaming missile into the air, careful to avoid the frosted branches.

With a roar, the bear's massive head swung around.

"Yeah, Paddington, now we're in business," Royce shouted, gripping part of his unbuttoned parka and spreading it wide, making himself appear as big as possible.

Bears usually preferred easy prey, so looking large could help scare him off. But he wasn't counting on it. He kept the shotgun in hand even as he held

his coat open. "Yeah, you. Back off, Baloo." Who
knew there were so many jolly bears in literature?
Kids should be taught to steer clear of them, not
cuddle the creatures. "There's no food in my trash,
and that little lady there isn't going to be dinner."

Or an appetizer, or canapé even, given the woman
appeared to be more of a wiry sort.

The car horn pierced the air, long and loud, as the
woman pressed the hell out of it. She had some serious mojo. No diving under the dashboard in fear
for herself. She revved the engine, puffing thicker
exhaust into the cold.

As the driver's side window eased down, a head
peeked out. That pink parka shone, hood up, but a
coal-dark ponytail trailed free along her shoulder.
"I'm trying to back up, but either the tires are stuck
or the bear weighs too—"

"Get back in there before Winnie the Pooh takes
off your head with one swipe of the paw," Royce
barked. Quick calculations told him he needed to get
that bear away from the SUV within the next two to
three minutes or the windshield would almost certainly shatter. The grizzly was big, but not too big
to climb through the busted front glass.

"Of course I'm going to stay in the car," she
shouted back. "I just wanted to know if you can think
of something I should be doing differently. I have
no intention of budging until Winnie-the-Pooh bear
trundles back off into the Hundred Acre Wood—"

The bear's paw swiped off the side mirror, inches

from her face. Fat snowflakes quickly piled on top of the shattered mirror, covering it in a testament to the power and fury of the Alaskan storm. Also, a reminder that Royce was up against more than just a grizzly.

Squealing, the woman tucked back into the SUV as the bear rolled off the vehicle and landed on the ground. On both back feet, wobbling but not down and not retreating.

No more playing around.

Royce raised his shotgun.

Aimed.

The SUV lurched backward, then forward, snow spewing. Apparently, the bear's weight had been keeping it in place, after all. Royce's shot went wild and the four-wheel drive skidded on the icy ground inches past him. The gleaming silver SUV was on a fast track to bashing into his igloo hideaway.

Royce launched to the left, out of the vehicle's path, while keeping eyes on the grizzly. The bear lumbered off into the tangle of slick trees. Clearly Teddy-Baloo-Paddington-Winnie thought better of tangling with that pink parka.

Speaking of which.

Royce checked right and—thank God—found the SUV at a stop in a puffy snowbank, the horn silent at last. The driver? Already climbing out from behind the wheel. Apparently unscathed.

And not as wiry as he'd originally thought. She was petite, alright, but with just the right kind of curves showcased in ski pants and a parka cinched at the waist.

A cute-as-hell—but still unwelcome—vision.

Now that the bear was gone, suspicion burned more than the frostbite threatening his face. Royce had to wonder. What was this woman doing out here in the middle of nowhere?

And what did she want with him?

Naomi Steele resented playing the wilting flower for any man.

She'd been born in Alaska, was a quarter Inuit on her dead mother's side. Growing up, she and her sisters had learned about survival in her harsh and magnificent home state right alongside her brothers. She could have handled the bear on her own with the flare gun in her survival kit.

But letting Royce Miller save her offered a golden opportunity to slide under the man's radar.

Shading her eyes against the fast-setting sun, Naomi watched the ornery grizzly hike back into the woods and out of sight. She turned slowly, careful to give her boots traction on the snow.

And…whoa, sexy snowman.

She'd seen press releases about Royce Miller during her internet search. She'd even sat in on one of his lectures a month ago, knew about his work from her background check on him prior to driving to his remote getaway. But no portfolio full of head shots, data or even back row auditorium viewing could have prepared her for his up close charisma. He was so much more than broodingly handsome good looks. The appeal was more than his leanly muscle-bound body on display in that open parka. And yeah, he got bonus points for the thick dark hair a hint too long like he'd forgotten to get a haircut, tousled like he'd just gotten out of bed.

All enticing. Sure.

But it was his eyes that held her. Those windows to the soul. To the man. A man with laser-sharp intelligence in his deep brown gaze that pierced straight to the core of her and seemed to say, *Bring it, woman. I can keep up.*

Raw sexual attraction crackled so hot in the air she half expected icicles to start melting off the trees.

Normally, she would have welcomed the draw, the challenge. But talk about poor timing. She needed to focus on her mission to wrangle a way to use that brilliant mind of his for her family's company.

And she happened to be two months pregnant. Those teenage years fighting cancer had seemed surreal at times, but she'd frozen some of her eggs before treatment, just in case. Her oncology specialist had called on a counselor to help her through so many decisions during that frightening experience.

Now she was ready to be a mother. She was through waiting around for a mythical Mr. Perfect. She'd started this journey with her career as a lawyer and her connections to her family as a solid foundation, but she'd since had her world turned upside down. With her father's engagement and the two rival companies merging, everyone was fighting for a place. And just as she had when she was a child, she needed to prove her place. For her child. For her sister who'd died. She blinked back tears.

*Pregnancy hormones.*

Of course. That must be the explanation for her off-the-charts reaction to a total stranger.

That stud muffin stranger adjusted his hold on the shotgun. "Let's get inside to talk before the bear comes back—or we're buried in a snowdrift."

"Oh, yeah, right." Another second staring at him and she could well have drool freeze to her face. She needed a level head to stay one step ahead of him. Royce wasn't just smart. He was genius smart—and eccentric.

Locating the recluse at all had taken Herculean detective work, employing the best of the best private investigators she'd used in her legal practice.

Detectives known for their discretion.

If the search gained her access to his pipeline research, it would be worth every penny. If she could somehow accomplish the unimaginable and persuade this lone ranger researcher to sign on with her family's oil company, well, that coup would be worth more than any amount of money.

She would finally win her family's full approval by contributing more than her legal advice to the business. She needed this for herself and for her child, a stable future. Strategy mattered more.

Royce opened the door to the glass igloo—and a beast of another kind came bounding out. A huge Saint Bernard leaned into him, sniffing, taking in all the surroundings. The air was heavy with scents of pine, the lingering smell of the spent flare gun still carried on the blizzard breeze.

"Tessie," Royce commanded in a soft rumble, "inside, girl."

Panting, the Saint Bernard shifted away from the front stoop and let them enter.

Bracing a hand against the door frame for balance, Naomi glanced around the space and found it much like ones her family had vacationed in over the years. God, those were amazing memories, a time before her mother and sister had died in a plane crash. Before Naomi had gotten cancer. A time she'd innocently thought could last forever. But those times had ended prematurely, like a short Alaskan day.

She looked upward, tipping her face toward the sun's rays. The igloo's glass dome let in the last beams of light. Only one wall was opaque, a wall with a platform bed against it, and almost certainly the bathroom and closet tucked cubicle-style behind.

Half the room had a long, curved sofa along the glass. Tessie had taken up residence on the couch, watching Naomi and Royce with wide brown eyes. The rest of the room held a kitchenette and dining table that was currently being used as a computer desk. No doubt, the keys to his research kingdom were inside that computer. Not that she expected him to have anything less than the best security.

"So?"

Royce Miller's voice pulled her back around.

"Yes, well…" She searched for the right words. She'd spent so much time figuring out how to find him and get here, she hadn't given much thought to being here. With him. Alone. "Thank you so much for saving my life."

He unloaded the shotgun with a swift efficiency that shouted his Texas upbringing, and pocketed the ammo. "What in the hell coerced you to venture out in this storm?"

"Whoa, hostility check, big guy. Is that any way to speak to the person who brought your supplies?" she asked with the charm that had won over dozens of tough-as-nails juries. "Without my trek up here, you could have starved, not to mention run out of deodorant."

"Supplies?" He eyed her warily, shrugging out of his parka and shaking the snow onto the doormat.

He made flannel look good.

But she ignored that and kept talking. "Yes, that's what I said. You have contracted a delivery service for your supplies while you're isolated up here." And she'd slipped the driver a hefty tip to let her bring the supplies up to her supposed boyfriend. The driver had been an old softie, a real romantic, and was easily persuaded. Lawyer skills with word craft came in handy out of the courtroom too. "And I'm here to restock your pantry. I thought I'd left in time to beat the storm, but it came on faster and heavier than expected. And, well, here I am."

Sure, she'd quibbled, insinuating she worked for the rental company's supply business. Truth be told, she hadn't outright said so. She could talk her way around that equivocation later. Because if he knew she was a part of the oil mogul Steele family, he would have likely left her to the bear.

"And you are?"

"Naomi." She said just her first name carefully, toying with her parka zipper. Then catching the nervous twitch, she stopped. No outright lies to backtrack from, she reminded herself.

She studied his face closely to see if her name sparked even a hint of recognition. Nope. Nothing. She didn't doubt her read of him. She'd been top of her law school class and had yet to lose a courtroom battle.

"Naomi, thank you for the supplies that you drove here in the middle of a blizzard," he said tightly, "but what do you expect to do now?"

"I expect for us to unload the supplies in my car before things freeze."

Sighing, he reached for his parka and started toward the door. "Have a seat. I'll get everything."

She raised a manicured hand. "Don't forget the flare gun in case our 'friend' returns."

"Got it."

"I can back you up with the shotgun if needed,"

she added, already sensing he would insist *no, no* and *hell no*.

He paused at the door, hand on the knob. "I've got it," he repeated, then stepped outside.

Ah, and just as predicted, he'd assumed she was as defenseless as she looked. For a smart man, he had a weakness and she'd found it fast.

He coddled women.

Some would think that rocked, and soak it right up. But she valued her independence. Her strength.

Her health.

She'd fought hard for her life, battling cancer as a teen, then battling all over again to elbow free of her family's overprotective ways. And yes, she'd gone overboard at times asserting herself, pushing through boundaries, which gained her a wild child reputation. She'd been bold. She'd partied and lived every day to the fullest. And she'd let her reputation become larger than life, more risqué than reality.

A choice that was coming back to bite her now that she genuinely gave a damn about being a part of the family business.

Speaking of which, she needed to get her butt in gear before Royce returned. This window of time while he was unloading the supplies was precious. She could recon his cabin. She would need every clue at her disposal to get past his defenses.

# Two

Head ducked into the wind that was picking up speed and throwing icy dartcicles, Royce carried the last box inside—his fifth trip. This Naomi was one hell of a delivery person. He had enough to make it through an apocalypse. Or thereabouts.

Frankly, the hauling—while done on a day colder than the coldest day in hell—had given him a chance to air out his thoughts regarding this unexpected turn of events at a time when he needed unwavering focus.

A visitor at his private retreat. A woman.

A drop-dead gorgeous woman.

He stepped back inside, his dog there to greet him with a nudge of the nose and wag of the tail.

Wide brown eyes seemed to ask about this new addition to their haven. Royce didn't have an answer yet. But he would.

"Hey," he said, "last box."

"Sorry the weather stinks so badly." She stood at the kitchen cabinets with the other boxes at her feet, unloading canned milk.

Naomi's parka was long gone and…damn, she was a sight for hungry eyes in formfitting jeans with silver studs and a red fuzzy sweater that all but shouted, *I'm soft—touch me.* Her dark ponytail swished in a silky glide as she reached upward to slide the can in place, then ducked back down to unload a jar of granola.

*Eyes off her ass.*

He set the last box on one of the two kitchen chairs, cushioned with leather for comfort and the kind of chair that could be used in his office or in the living area. Everything in the space was efficient and multipurpose. "Isn't someone going to be worried when you don't return?"

"I texted one of my brothers while you were outside." She wriggled her toes in thick socks, stacking cans to make room for the granola container.

Texted? "How did you manage that? The signal up here sucks."

Sure, *he* could call out and email, but his equipment was top-of-the-line with a portable minisatellite dish.

"I have a really good phone," she answered simply over her shoulder, inky-black ponytail stroking along her back in a way that made him consider what it would feel like to trace her hair's path, then test the texture in a gentle fist.

"That's advanced tech equipment for a delivery person."

Stepping down, she faced him, smile bright, her full lips glistening with fresh gloss. "My family's generous. And, um, I was helping a friend by making the delivery since they were overwhelmed with storm purchases." She tugged at the hem of her red sweater, a slight flush staining her cheeks. "I don't actually work for the supply shop."

"You're a good friend, then, to make a trip in this weather." He still wasn't sure why he couldn't accept she was here to bring his supplies. It just seemed off that the store would send a woman out alone in this crazy-monstrous spring blizzard to deliver paper towels and canned goods. He should call, just to verify, which he would as soon as the supply offices reopened tomorrow...or after the storm.

A deep, shining smile plumped her cheeks, eyes dancing in the warm light. "We all have our reasons for doing things. Friendship is a treasure   and a hefty motivator."

"True enough." His parents and their next-door neighbors had been best friends, like family.

They'd been thrilled when Royce had started dating their friends' daughter, the girl next door, whose father worked alongside his. His parents hadn't been as excited when she got pregnant, since a baby would have changed his plans for a PhD. However, wedding preparations ensued...until a pipeline explosion rocked the town. His fiancée's father died.

Then his fiancée miscarried the baby.

Before Royce could process the grief over losing his child, Carrie Lynn had broken the engagement and left. For good.

Life fell apart for him. He didn't give himself over to emotion easily. It wasn't in his nature. Figuring out how to recover from that loss ten years ago had been tougher than anything he'd faced in his life.

But Royce had pieced himself back together with an unwavering focus on work and a dedication to reducing the chances of a pipeline tragedy happening to any other family again. Hell, he was better off doing what he did best.

Dealing with science and facts, not emotions and feelings.

His passion for his work had cost him relationships, but damn it, he wasn't interested in changing himself or his values for anyone.

Take him as he was. Period.

So, in reality, this woman wasn't a threat beyond being a physical temptation.

Reassured for the moment, he stepped out of his boots, his wool socks much like hers. Except his weren't purple.

Naomi closed the cabinet and settled in an empty

chair, crossing her legs, purple-socked foot swinging. "Are you vacationing?"

"Working." A fact that shouldn't require elaboration.

She laughed lightly. "You don't look like a professional ice fisherman."

"I'm not."

"Then what are you working on?" she asked, drumming her fingers on his laptop computer, his abacus key chain resting beside on the table. "Your memoirs of life in the Alaskan wilds fighting bears?"

"Nosy much?" He moved the final box of supplies to the floor and sat in the other chair, eyeing her.

"I'm just making polite conversation. Unless you're going to cue up Netflix, we have time to kill waiting out the storm."

Damn, she was funny and sassy as well as hot. How long was this storm supposed to last?

"I have an extensive library on my tablet. You're welcome to browse. Make yourself comfortable over there on the sofa."

Out of his workspace and far enough away so that he wouldn't be breathing in the crisp scent of her, something like—he sought an intellectual answer to such an elemental scent—like the water, the ocean. Icy salt air. Did they make that into a perfume or was it just the scent of her? He focused back in on her words.

"While you work at…"

"I'm a science professor." He tossed out his generic answer, a truth. He did give the periodic guest lecture series.

"So, you have papers to grade?" she pushed without budging from her seat.

"Hmm…" He pulled his tablet out of his computer bag and cued up the library, while making sure the rest of his data was tightly password protected.

"You're not the chatty sort."

"Nope."

"You were talkative earlier, with the bear." She toyed with her ponytail, shiny black strands gliding through her fingers.

"Adrenaline." A chemical currently pumping through his body again as he watched her play with her hair. Was it his imagination or was she flirting?

And if she was, did he want to take her up on that offer?

*Hell, yes.*

She reached across the small teak table. "Is the offer for that tablet full of reading material still available?"

Three hours later, stars glinting overhead and a fire crackling in the stone hearth, Naomi curled up with a blanket and throw pillows, pretending to be engrossed in a mystery novel on the glowing tablet. She'd already read it a week ago, so if Royce asked questions, she would be able to answer. Meanwhile, she could study him and figure out how best to proceed.

Upon reflection, Naomi wasn't so sure this plan

had been her best. After receiving the investigator's report, she'd moved quickly. Usually a strength of hers. Fast decision-making.

But given the upheaval in her family lately, she had to admit, she wasn't at the top of her game.

She'd rushed up here without considering all the outcomes.

Gathering a look at Royce's data would be easier said than done, and a few notes here and there would only have short-term benefits. Persuading him to join forces with the Steele and Mikkelson family businesses, which were merging into Alaska Oil Barons, was going to be a challenge. Especially with the tumultuous press her family had been generating since her dad had announced his surprise engagement to the Mikkelson widow—Jeannie. Stock prices had dropped.

Then her brother had gotten engaged to a Mikkelson and they were parenting a baby together.

Boom. No warning.

Stock prices dipped again. The board of directors rumbled there was too much chaos, too much emotional fallout and not enough strategy. They weren't sure how the merger would play out, and the board hated uncertainty.

She wasn't so sure she disagreed with them. She trusted her family. But the Mikkelsons? She'd been raised to consider them the enemy. Had that feud ended just because their patriarch had died? Could the entire contentious atmosphere be blamed on one person?

Not likely.

She needed to solidify her role in the company. She was keeping a close eye on things from a legal perspective, but she'd need to win as many allies as possible to act on any discrepancies she found. She didn't know how the rival companies would be blended or how leadership positions would be divided. Nabbing Royce Miller for her family's team would go a long way in garnering loyalty and upping her professional profile.

But she would be a fool to think she could accomplish that tonight. She would settle in and watch his body language; she'd wait for that moment when he started to relax. Another courtroom tactic with a practical application.

Her stomach rumbled, reminding her how little she'd eaten. She'd only managed a few crackers in the morning and a cup of soup at lunch.

Now? She was ravenous. Yes, she had a job to do here with Royce, but she also needed to take care of her baby and keep track of what she ate. With her finicky taste buds lately, it was all too easy to skip eating until she was nearly dizzy, like now.

Setting aside the tablet, she stood and made her way to the kitchenette, sidestepping the table where Royce tapped away at his computer. He glanced up just as she opened the minifridge.

Royce tipped back in his chair, eyeing her with heavy-lidded dark eyes. "That's my food."

"I'll be glad to pay for my portion of this pudding cup and pear." She tossed the fruit in the air and caught it with a quick snap. "We're stranded. Do you intend to let me starve—or make me freeze out there ice fishing?"

He chuckled softly, a whiskey rich sound. "If you're hungry, help yourself to anything in the pantry."

"I am starving, actually. Bear hunting is quite exhausting." She crunched a bite of the pear and searched for a spoon. "Can I make you something, to earn my keep and all? I imagine grading papers is tiring."

"I'm fine. I ate earlier." He toyed with his abacus key chain, thumbing the beads back and forth. "Thank you though."

Inspiration struck and she sliced the pear instead. Suddenly, scooping the slices through the chocolate pudding sounded five-star awesome. Her taste buds seemed to vacillate between "no way" and "oh my God good," these days.

Settling across from him again, she scooped and crunched, savored and watched. A lot of oh my God good for the senses around this place.

Sighing, he finally met her gaze. "What?"

Blinking fast, she smiled widely. "Sorry. Am I bothering you?"

"I'm used to working alone, in quiet." His gaze homed in on her snack plate.

"Sorry the snowstorm didn't accommodate. Truly. It could be days, so honestly, it will be easier if we make nice, perhaps talk a bit. You can't work *all* the time."

He closed his computer again and scooped up the key chain. "Fine. Let's talk. Aren't you worried I'm a serial killer?"

In a whisper, she asked, trying to ease him into a conversation. Tease him a bit. She had enough brothers to know this tactic would probably work. "Are you?"

"My answer isn't going to matter." The abacus beads clicked under his fingers. "You know that, right?"

He had a point, but he didn't know she wasn't operating blind here. She wouldn't be able to carry this off long without risking alienating him altogether. "I'm an incredibly insightful person."

"From meeting so many people at work."

She looked up sharply. "Yes, actually."

"Well, lucky for you, I'm not a serial killer. I'm just an antisocial scientist."

"That must be tough to maintain in the classroom, Professor."

"Works fine in a lecture hall." He set his key chain down again.

Her mind zipped back to the first time she'd heard him speaking to an auditorium full of students and even professionals who'd joined the class to hear him. He saw the oil industry through revolutionary eyes. He walked a difficult line in making all sides of the spectrum happy, upping production while finding ways to increase safety and decrease ecological impact. His brain was every bit as sexy as his body.

O-kay.

Her distraction level was peaking.

She shot to her feet, tossed her empty pudding cup in the trash and popped the last slice of pear into her mouth.

"I thought you were going to eat and read?"

"I think I'm just going to turn in. Since you're not a serial killer." She winked.

He lifted an eyebrow. "Do you need some sweats?"

"I think I'll be fine in my thermal leggings and undershirt. Although I may need to take you up on that offer of sweats tomorrow when wash time comes." Guilt tugged at her. She really wasn't playing fair. "Thank you for being so nice about letting me stay here."

"Don't be so quick to thank me. I may not be a serial killer, but that doesn't mean I'm giving up my bed for you."

And there he went being funny again, like with his litany against the bear. "I didn't ask you to give me your bed."

Although she couldn't deny the raw attraction crackling tangibly in the air. The fire of it filled her mind with images of sharing that bed with him.

Something must have flickered in her eyes because his widened, then narrowed, holding hers.

His head tipped to the side.

Nerves tingled along her skin, an unusual occurrence. She wasn't one to back down. Ever.

Perhaps she could call this a retreat. She swallowed, trying to recover from the heat in his dark eyes. "The sofa's more than fine. Thank you."

His chair legs lowered to all four on the floor again. "It's okay, Naomi. Take the bed. I'll be working late, anyway."

"But—"

The words died on her lips as he shook his head. "My mama wouldn't have it any other way. Manners and all. I'll sack out on the sofa. Good night, Naomi."

Good night?

Sleep felt like the furthest thing possible.

Naomi woke up, legs tangled in the tan satin comforter.

It was dark overhead, but that didn't mean anything in Alaska. She checked her watch and…holy cow. It was already five in the morning. She'd slept for nearly nine hours, out like a log. She shoved her hair back from her face.

When would she get used to these pregnancy hormones owning her body?

She was grateful for her baby, but she sure hadn't expected so many physical changes in a couple of months. Slowly, she sat up, wary, but her stomach stayed steady.

Scanning the studio area, she looked for Royce but found the space empty except for the dog snoozing under the table. The computer was nowhere in sight. Apparently, Royce wasn't leaving it unattended any longer.

Behind the wall that housed the headboard, she heard the shower running. That explained where her "roomie" was. And even though they'd both been in and out of the bathroom area last night, this was different. Thinking of him there, without his clothes, in that tiled shower sent a tingle down her spine clear to her toes.

She needed to distract herself. Pronto.

Naomi flipped back the covers, her fleece-lined leggings and undershirt soft against her skin. Thank goodness Alaskan weather meant layers. That left her with extra clothes while she stayed here longer than she'd expected.

She would sneak a call to her brother while she had privacy. Her backpack held the basics, just enough to seem normal on a day trip, and she refused to vainly wish for her closet full of clothes and makeup.

Focus.

She fished out her phone with the booster signal and dialed up her oldest brother, Broderick. With their dad in the throes of new love and planning a wedding, Broderick had become the de facto head of their family with orders from their father to make peace. Their dad had demanded that the Steeles and Mikkelsons unite as a family and a company. Get along—or sell their shares and move on.

Broderick had been charged with aligning the finances of the two companies, along with rival CFO Glenna Mikkelson. They'd surprised everyone by resuming their brief college romance…and now they were engaged and raising Glenna's daughter together.

If Broderick and Glenna could balance romance and work, why couldn't her father and his new "girlfriend" tend to the business angle, or at least participate more in the transition? The rest of them were barely treading water keeping up with the abrupt changes, keeping board members calm— and watching their backs as siblings on either side of the merged family jockeyed for top-dog position. The only Mikkelson son who seemed to be out of the running was Trystan, who managed their family's ranch and insisted he wanted no part of anything that required a suit.

Naomi kept one ear on the shower and another on the phone. The call rang and rang, then went to voice mail. She tried again with no luck.

Looking at the one bar of connectivity, she knew her chance to phone out could be limited. Sighing, she quickly dialed her sister Delaney. She wasn't as in-your-face as their brother about the business. But Delaney had a stubborn streak a mile long, especially when it came to ecological protection.

Perhaps her sister should have been her first call instead of Broderick.

Two rings in, Delaney picked up. "How's it going?"

Naomi wandered to the curved sofa lining part of the igloo wall for a better vantage point to monitor the bathing area for the second Royce stepped out. "I'm getting to know him. But he's not chatty. His dog's a better conversationalist."

Her sister laughed lightly. "But you're talking to the great Dr. Royce Miller. That's more than anyone else has managed to accomplish. I'm impressed."

"I've got crazy-good lawyering skills." She injected punch in her tone, more than she was feeling. She was fading fast energywise. What a strange, unexpected turn her expedition here had taken.

"That you do."

"Was that an actual compliment?" Naomi teased, relaxing into the familiarity of a normal conversation with her sister. She was lucky to have a large family, three brothers and a sister. They were such a great support.

And as she thought of her family, she couldn't help but think of her mother and her sister Brea, who were gone. Losing them had left such a hole in her heart—and a need for stability.

"Hey, was that insecurity, Naomi?" Delaney's tone was anything but teasing. More like stunned.

Few knew that shy Delaney had far more fight in her than Naomi did. Delaney chewed up corporate types who showed disregard for the environment.

Delaney's latest target for scathing letters to the editors had been bigwig investor Birch Montoya, which did prove a bit problematic since the family business could use his financial endorsement, especially if they were to take on something as big as making Royce Miller's style of changes.

*If* Naomi won Royce Miller.

"Insecurity?" Not that she would admit. "Never. It's just nice to hear affirmation." Especially at a time when she was questioning herself. So many changes. So many hormones. And she still had to face telling her family about the pregnancy. "Things are strange in the family right now. How were Dad and Jeannie at dinner last night? Sorry to have crashed early." Pregnancy had made her so sleepy.

"Dad and Jeannie are the same. They're like teenagers planning their wedding. Not that they're waiting on the ceremony. That day Glenna and Broderick found them in the shower togeth—"

"Stop," Naomi said fast, half laughing. "My brain is on fire with the image."

"Imagine if we'd actually been there." Delaney chuckled softly, then the sound dwindled. "The thing that's starting to get to me though…if this was our mom and dad, we would think it was romantic. Granted, no one needs the full Monty."

"Can you please stop with the naked references?" Her eyes drifted back to the shower area. To Royce. There was a sauna there too. Oh, the possibilities heated her thoughts.

Her warm forehead rested against the cool glass wall. Lights around the property barely pierced the blizzard.

"I never would have pegged you for a prude."

Ouch, that stung, not that she intended to let Delaney know. "Well, it's not like you're in the middle of some torrid affair, either."

Silence stretched between them.

Putting Naomi on alert. She straightened. "Are you?"

"My love life is tame. I'm too busy with work. You're just imaging things after all that time you spent helping your friend revamp online dating profiles."

Naomi sensed something in her sister's voice beyond the simple teasing, but with a crackly cell phone reception, perhaps now wasn't the best time to push on personal stuff. Though she couldn't deny she was curious. "How're things going with smoothing Birch Montoya's ruffled feathers?"

"I'm working on it. It's just…not that simple for me. I feel like we would be taking money from the devil, given his stance on protecting the environment."

"Then that makes it all the more important for me to bring Royce on board to balance things out." Naomi chewed her lip for a moment before adding, "It's all so complicated."

"The business as much as the family." Delaney's words carried a hefty sigh. "It's not that I don't want

Dad to move on. I'm just having trouble with him choosing a life with *her*."

And from all indications, Jeannie Mikkelson's kids were having a difficult time with the shocker romance, as well. Sure, Jeannie's husband had been dead for two years—of a heart attack. But the families had been at war for so long. So many harsh words and character assassinations had taken place. And the gossip. Someone went so far as to hint the Mikkelsons had played a part in the fatal plane crash that killed Brea and their mother—completely unsubstantiated and unbelievable. But investors were going to find it tough to overlook divisions so deep and public.

Naomi toyed with a lock of her hair. "Broderick is marrying a Mikkelson. Are you saying that's a problem?"

"I'm just saying it's not easy."

Back in college, Broderick and Glenna had indulged in a poorly hidden brief affair, then split up. Glenna had married someone else and become a widow before reuniting with Broderick very recently.

"And now they have a precious baby." A baby conceived when Glenna's husband had an affair shortly before he came down with pancreatic cancer and died. And yet, Glenna and Broderick still loved Fleur unconditionally. They were in the process of making the adoption official after the baby had been abandoned by her mother.

Naomi's hand slid over her stomach and she wondered if her child would have a father's love someday.

"Fleur's pretty awesome." The smile in Delaney's voice was unmistakable. "You should see her wave her fists. I'm certain she's bumping my fist on purpose."

"Of course she is," Naomi joked right back. "Sing her an extra lullaby from Aunt Naomi."

"You can't carry a tune."

"That's why you're going to sing it for me." The shower silenced in the bathroom. Naomi's heart did a flip against her rib cage. She really needed a game plan for dealing with the sexy scientist before he emerged. "Gotta go now. Love you."

She thumbed her phone off fast and bent over to shove it in her backpack, making sure the security code locked the screen. The hair on the back of her neck prickled, as if she was being watched. She checked the dog, but Tessie was sound asleep and snoring which could only mean...

Naomi straightened slowly and turned to find Royce. Big and awake and sexy, he stood in low-slung sweatpants, towel-drying his hair. He watched her with so much heat in his eyes, she barely resisted the urge to drag a finger down the glass windows to check for steamy condensation.

Delaney Steele had a secret.

Sliding the cell phone into her coat pocket, she hoped what she'd been doing—was about to do again—wouldn't wreck her sister's plan with Royce Miller.

But she just couldn't bring herself to tell Naomi.

Stepping out of her SUV into the snowy parking lot, Delaney braced herself for the walk into the Steele family headquarters. Wind whipped hard off the mountains, bringing a frosty bite against her cheek until she yanked up the deep hood of her parka.

Maybe Delaney was too adept at keeping things hidden, until it just became instinct. Such as how she wasn't as shy as she pretended to be. Or how she'd kissed her sister's boyfriend in high school. Or that she was scared of everyone's dogs, but didn't want to hurt their feelings.

Or how she fought survivor's guilt every day of her life.

She'd pretended to have the flu before the fateful flight that had shattered her family. Her mother had discovered the faked fever. Delaney had begged her mom not to go. Silly really. She'd just wanted her to stay to go shopping for makeup. Naomi had offered to accompany Delaney instead. Case closed.

Their mom and sister, Brea, had left for the flight—late. If they'd been on time...

What-ifs could rule a life.

Messenger bag tucked under her arm, Delaney put her head down and trudged forward, boots crunching through the icy crust that no amount of salting and shoveling could clear on mornings like this one. Forward was the only way she knew, after all.

These days, with so many regrets, she lived each day determined to grasp what she wanted and not add a single new item to that list. So hell no, she wasn't even close to being the crusader, the good girl her family believed. She'd only wanted to somehow make a mark, somehow help other families not suffer the pain hers had experienced.

She just hoped her current secret didn't torpedo all of Naomi's careful plans. Because Delaney was in so deep now, she wasn't sure she could stop herself if she tried.

# Three

Royce never would have imagined silk thermals on a woman could look sexier than any lingerie.

Not that he could think of any woman other than Naomi at the moment. This one was filling his every thought.

Which wasn't a wise idea when they would be sharing a one-room studio igloo-cabin for an undetermined amount of time. It wasn't like he could jog off his pent-up sexual tension outside. The snowstorm was still raging. Even getting his dog to make the requisite "nature's breaks" outdoors was tough. Tessie bolted out into the igloo tunnel, had her moment and sprinted back into the shelter in record time. She shook snowflakes off her shaggy coat, creating a mini flurry indoors.

Too bad they couldn't all just hibernate.

Last night, he'd kept his eyes averted when Naomi had come out of the restroom, because just the sound of her movements, the scent of her, was distraction enough. And yes, once he'd given up and stretched out on the sofa, he'd watched her sleep. The covers had been pulled up to her shoulders, but the moonlight had played over her face.

It had been a long time since he'd slept with a woman. More than a year. There were offers, but lately work had consumed his life. He didn't have time for a relationship. This was a turning point in his research, everything coming together at just the right time.

To be honest, he was racing to finalize his work because the Alaskan pipeline production through Canada and into the Dakotas would ramp up sooner rather than later. If anything, the Steele-Mikkelson merger had accelerated the program since their major Alaskan competitor, Johnson Oil United, was sending signals of speeding their plans while the Steele-Mikkelsons were preoccupied with the merger.

And the more the businesses raced against each other, the more Royce worried. This wasn't the type of industry to rush, and the Johnsons already showed some hints of corner cutting. Even minuscule miscalculations could prove deadly or leave long-lasting contamination concerns. He couldn't afford distractions.

And no question, this woman was a major distraction.

There was something about Naomi…something he couldn't identify that tugged at him, a feeling that he couldn't shake. That there was more than met the eye with her. In a good or bad way? He didn't know.

Although he did know he needed to be on his toes around her until he figured her out.

He looped the towel around the doorknob and reached for his Massachusetts Institute of Technology—MIT—sweatshirt, mulling over the best way to learn more about her. He needed to find a chink in that spunky facade, to see who she was on the inside and discover if a quirk of fate had truly brought her here. Or if there might be another reason she was holed up with him. Regardless, she intrigued him.

Tugging on the thick fleece, he stepped deeper into the room, aware of her sharp, analytic eyes. "So, you grew up in Alaska?"

"I did." She curled her toes in her socks and sat on the edge of the sofa.

"Could you have handled that bear on your own?"

"Maybe. Okay, probably," she said, smiling, her nose crinkling, knees bouncing nervously. "But I enjoyed watching you take over."

"How magnanimous of you." His dry tone cut her smile. She exchanged it for a wink before readjusting on the couch, a shift that revealed her curves more fully.

"Your ego seems solid." She looked at him squarely, but her twitching increased.

He dropped to sit at the end of the sofa, searching her deep brown eyes. "What's really going on here with you showing up?"

She stared back for a solid, sparking sixty seconds or so before shooting to her feet. "I have to go to the restroom."

And just that fast, she bolted away, the bathroom door slamming and locking behind her.

Naomi had never been so glad to take advantage of a pregnancy symptom.

She had to use the bathroom at least twice as often these days, which made the one-facility situation here a tricky element she hadn't considered in driving up to the secluded cabin. But as Royce had pressed her with questions, she'd been glad for the excuse to leave the room.

Brushing away morning breath went a long way too in clearing her sleep-fogged mind. Now that she'd had time to fully wake up, she had a plan.

She had decided to take a calculated risk.

Royce was a man of logic, a scientist. So, she intended to throw him for a loop, knock him off balance. Opting for outrageous remarks had worked well for her in the past in getting people to say things they might not have otherwise. And then with laugh-

ter and the sharing of even a little secret, they relaxed, revealing more as the rapport strengthened.

Such a tactic might well work in her favor now.

Naomi left the bathroom cubicle and leaned
against the archway leading into the studio area.
Royce moved efficiently in the kitchen, cooking
bacon, sausage, and popping large slices of fresh
wheat bread onto a toaster slab that fit in the fireplace.

Her mouth watered and her senses tingled on high
alert. Because of her pregnancy or because of the
man?

She reminded herself of her mission. She tugged
the hem of her boring thermal shirt and asked,
"Wanna play strip poker? I'll trade you clothes for
first dibs on that food."

He glanced over his broad shoulder. "Do you always proposition strangers?"

"Only you." She fluffed her dark hair, a seductive
challenge in her subtle moves.

He turned his attention back to the meal at hand.
Unfazed. A low, rumbling chuckle. "Ah, you're being
outrageous to get me to stop thinking and reveal—
something?—to you."

He was smart, quick-witted, not easily fooled.
"Very insightful."

"So sarcastic." Facing him, she couldn't help
but notice the solidity of his chest beneath his MIT
sweatshirt.

"But you're talking to me now rather than hiding

behind your computer." He raised one brow and for a moment, almost too brief to register, a flicker of amusement danced across her face, smiling, bowing in…interest?

Dragging his attention from her back to the breakfast food seemed to be no easy task. He scrambled and flipped the eggs once more. His hands moved with such precision, the mark of a man with an ingrained attention to detail. Her mouth dried up at the vision of those hands paying precise attention along her body.

"True enough." He stalked quietly toward the kitchen area, pulling out plates for each item.

His eyes met hers, and there it was—that pop of electricity, something warming her to her core. The fluttering in her stomach intensified. Not pregnancy related, but a reminder of what her future held.

Royce dumped the sausage links and bacon onto a plate, arranged them neatly in a row. He fished out the four pieces of freshly toasted bread. The yeasty smell mixed with the savory smell of bacon and sausage.

He met her gaze, held it before he spoke. "Keep your clothes. I could stand a big breakfast too. What do you want to discuss?"

Naomi scratched just behind her ear, collecting her cool after spending even more time drooling over the man than the food. Deciding her strategy as he set out fresh jams on the small counter in front of

her. The spread was vast, especially given their min-
imalist setting.

Bacon, sausage links, fluffy eggs, toast. All things
she didn't even realize she was craving until now.
Might as well feed one hunger pulsing through her
and hopefully rein her thoughts in.

Tilting her head, she continued, "Since strip poker
didn't get a rip-roaring endorsement, let's go with
something more practical." She sat back on the edge
of the bed and hugged her knees. "I would enjoy
hearing more about your work."

"I told you. I'm a science professor." His smile
was taut, tense.

And his response? Vague as ever.

But his eyes sparked with something else when
she held his gaze. Her pulse quickened…at the game
of wits or at something else entirely?

Food. She needed to eat.

"Well I figured you weren't a communications
professor. Science is a broad field though. Care to
narrow it down a bit? I assume you're passionate
about your career given how intensely you concen-
trate."

With a sigh, he piled food on his plate. She
watched him close his eyes, seeming to weigh his
next words carefully. What felt like an eternity
passed before he spoke again. His low voice a welcome rumble.

"I'm an engineer, actually. I work on oil pipeline
construction and upgrades."

"A mathematical as well as scientific field. Interesting. What do you enjoy most about the pipeline angle? I'm having fun envisioning you out there in the wilds, the bear master flexing his intellectual chops."

"Still nosy." A smile—well, a half smile—pulled at his lips. He arranged the spread on the table, down to the precise position of both of their plates. He gestured for her to join him.

"Why does it matter if I know what you do?" She walked over to the table, settling into the seat closest to the glass. The snow still poured down, muting the minimal rays of sunrise, giving the breakfast a hazy, romantic glow.

Brushing knees with him under the table only added to the intimacy.

"I've shared with you," he dodged. She reached for the toast and then scrambled eggs as he continued, an edge of sarcasm tinging his tone. "Tell me more about being a delivery gal. How long have you had the job? Why did you apply to drive around in awful weather? Why did they hire you?"

"I told you, I'm a friend." Stick with rule number one: keep the story as simple and unadorned as possible. Too many details would complicate things. She tucked her knees closer to her side of the table. "I volunteered to help him out."

"Ah, right." He shoveled a large bite of eggs into his mouth.

Either he wasn't listening to her or he was trying

to trip her up, which meant he was suspicious. With good reason.

Guilt pinched. Hard. He seemed to be a genuinely good guy and she wasn't being totally up-front with him. It had all seemed so simple back home, the stakes for her family so high. And none of that had changed. She wanted security for her baby and she believed in her cause. She wasn't as active as her sister on the issue of the environment, but her family's company truly was the one most open to what Royce had to offer.

Bottom line, she deeply believed research like Royce's helped reduce environmentally caused cancers, and the thought of saving others the grief she'd been through? She had to forge ahead.

"Tell me more about you? Family? Friends? Girlfriend who won't be happy to find out I've been here alone with you offering to play strip poker?"

"I'm an only child," he said, taking the bait as she shifted the topic. "My parents had me later in life and are retired. Girlfriends aren't your concern."

"Efficient answers. Sparse. But efficient."

Like he was with serving up portions on his plate from the platter in the middle.

"I grew up in Texas around the oil fields. My father and mother worked hard. We had a comfortable life. I studied hard and it paid off with a full ride to college. I made good with some patents, which enables me to afford to hide out working in a luxurious glass igloo and pay for delivery of supplies," he said simply, adding butter to his bread while it was still warm, the dab melting over the sides.

Kind of like her senses. He was eccentric, sure, but sexy as hell. The intensity in his eyes had disarmed her for a moment. She needed to press on while he was warming up into an unusually chatty mood.

"Texas to Alaska. That's quite a leap geographically, not to mention the weather."

"Oil. Pipelines. Common thread." He lifted his mug of coffee.

"Ah, yes. Oil."

"Hmm." He offered up the nonanswer while adding jam to his buttered toast.

She was losing him here. Or maybe she was losing focus, because all she could think about was him in the shower. His buff chest, his strong arms. "Tell me about your childhood growing up in Texas?"

He glanced at her, that strong jawline causing her heart to quicken. Something like a crackle of awareness passed between them, something that seemed to hang in the air. "Growing up in Texas was a lot like growing up in Alaska, I imagine, but without the snow."

"Since the snow is everywhere, how about spell it out for me more." She bit into her own toast, indulging in the freshness of the blueberry jam.

"Both places have fishing, hunting, rugged living…and oil."

"I applaud your concise way with words." And

yes, she was starting to struggle to keep her thoughts reined in with the sensory overload of savory food and muscle-bound man.

He shrugged one shoulder. "Concise."

Royce's attention wandered for a moment, eyes roving her, stopping at her mouth. His sudden movement caught her off guard as he reached across the table and thumbed the corner of her mouth. "Jam."

He slowly licked his thumb clean. But his eyes didn't leave hers.

Her heart did a flip. Her thoughts scattered like snow from the roof in a squall. So much for staying on her toes around him. About the only way she could envision being on her tiptoes involved arching up to kiss him.

Royce wasn't sure why he'd opted to play with fire by touching Naomi. But damned if he regretted it.

Angling across the table, he skimmed his mouth over the corner of her lips, right where he'd grazed her with his thumb a second before. The taste of jam lingered.

As did the spark of attraction as he settled back into his seat.

She hadn't objected. She wasn't running. Granted, she appeared a hint shell-shocked with wise eyes. But her pupils widened with attraction. She was stunning, potent.

And he was drawn to her like a magnet.

He studied her through narrowed eyes. "You're—distracting."

"I'm sorry about that." She sat back in the chair, and he couldn't help but notice the way her spine arched and her breasts pressed against her shirt.

*Distracting* was an understatement. His normally targeted linguistic skills seemed to fail him. She was…intoxicating. That might be more accurate.

"I didn't mean it in a bad way." He held her gaze, watching the way her lips moved, parting ever so slightly. The touch a moment ago, the taste of her, had left him wanting more. Much more.

"Oh, thank you." She exhaled hard. "Well, I guess there really isn't any use in denying the sparks, is there?"

Her bright eyes searched his, an eagerness dancing there. One he wanted to act on. Damn the logic.

"Attraction is what it is. Even my scientific mind knows it's not logical—but it is tangible." He leaned forward on the table, his knee brushing hers. She stared at the point of contact, the place where electricity seemed to build, coursing through him.

"I'm not a judgy kind of person." She lifted her head, fixating now on his mouth. But her knee didn't move from his. The warmth of her body teased him as she continued, her voice lower as if confessing a secret, "but I've also never indulged in a one-night stand."

"From the looks of the storm and the piles of snow out there, we'll be here for far more than one night.

If you're so inclined to…indulge." He eased from his chair and leaned a hip against the table, taking her hand, surprised for a moment by the softness of her skin, the strength in the way she squeezed him back.

"Logical point." Her breath hitched audibly, her pulse speeding in her neck just below her diamond stud earring.

Were they really discussing this without ever even having kissed other than sharing a smudge of jam?

Although holding her hand, watching her reaction to that simple touch, turned him inside out with need.

"And I am a responsible man. I always have protection."

Her husky laugh washed over him. "You carry condoms to an igloo in remote Alaska?"

"Did you hear me? I am a practical man. And a careful man." He paused, looking down at his feet before continuing, the words heavy on his tongue. "My former fiancée got pregnant. We lost the baby, then broke up. If I'd been careful, I could have saved us both a lot of pain…"

Her hand rested on the back of his neck. "I'm so sorry for the hurt that caused you."

"Thank you." Pushing back against the memories, he glanced up at her again. "It was a long time ago. And damn, I don't know why I brought it up at all. What a total mood buster. I just wanted to say that I have condoms."

"Safe is always good." Her fingers moved lightly along the back of his neck, both soothing and arousing.

His direct nature had sent him off course with people before, and he wondered if that was the case now. "So, have I totally wrecked the mood?"

"Wrecked the mood?" She angled back, toying with the tip of her ponytail in a way that totally set his senses on fire. Did she know what she was doing to him? "Dampened it perhaps. But I think the moment could be easily salvaged."

*Yes.* Victory surged through him. "How so?"

She gave him an unmistakably sultry look. All thick lashes and parted lips. She raised an eyebrow, voice taking on a sweeter intonation. "You're a smart man. Guess."

Angling toward her, he slid his hand up her leg, watching her move into him with anticipation. He drew his head closer, lips a breath apart from hers.

The logical stuff? He would deal with that later. Because right now, nothing seemed more important than fully, thoroughly kissing Naomi.

# Four

The moment Royce's lips fully brushed hers, Naomi leaned into the kiss, unable to stop herself from soaking up the muscular feel and earthy scent of this man she barely knew. Throwing herself at a virtual stranger. Which was atypical for her.

Sure, she'd cultivated a wild child reputation for the past few years. Totally unearned other than dressing flamboyantly and being outspoken. But she'd felt compelled somehow to prove to her family she was vibrantly alive. Independent. She'd even stopped waiting around for Mr. Right and embraced the possibility of motherhood.

And now when she was well out of the public eye, she was about to do the most reckless thing of her life jumping into bed with Royce Miller—who she should be winning over in a more practical fashion.

However, she was feeling anything but practical or logical at that moment.

The stroke of his tongue, the feel of his sure touch along her shoulders, down her back, brought her senses alive. Everything became more vibrant. The rasp of his beard-stubbled face. The coarse texture of his hair that she'd thought needed a cut and now found perfect. The smoky scent from the fireplace mingling with the musk of man.

His kiss was intoxicating.

Although, worry still niggled. What if sleeping with him compromised her goal of cajoling him into taking a job with Alaska Oil Barons, Incorporated? She certainly hadn't been able to snag so much as a peek at his work, which actually made her feel less guilty now. However, if they followed the attraction through, sex would complicate things. He might well believe she'd used sex as a means to persuade him.

Except damn, the draw between them was so tangible, undeniable. Hopefully he would know the truth of that.

If she revealed the truth of why she was there, this sexual exploration would end. She wanted to experience him first, no matter the consequences.

And she'd done so little real living with all those years devoted to recovering from cancer. Her future would be filled with putting her own needs aside for her child's welfare… This was a window of time for her to indulge in what she sensed would be a most memorable, delicious experience.

She was going to sleep with Royce Miller.

It was crazy on the one hand.

And totally logical on the other.

The attraction to Royce reached deep within her, and this could well be her only chance to pursue it. Once business officially intruded…

She had to seize this moment now.

Thankfully, he seemed to agree. Even Tessie somehow knew to grant them privacy and trotted off to curl up in her dog bed in the closet area.

Naomi gripped his fleecy sweatshirt in her hands. "This is insane."

"I know." He rested his forehead against hers, his breath ragged. "I apologize if I overstepped in moving so fast."

She laughed hoarsely. "I'm the one who mentioned strip poker."

He smiled, his fingers playing down her spine. "I'm the one who brought up condoms."

"You sure did." Her fists unfurled from his fleece and she palmed his chest. Oh my, his chest.

The desire in his eyes echoed the flame inside her. She wasn't sure who initiated what, who moved first. It was all a blur of motion and want. Her arms looped around his neck as he scooped her up, carrying her to the bed, lowering her with gentle strength. As he released her, his hand skimmed around her hips, grazing her stomach.

Her heart lurched to her throat for an instant as she thought of her pregnancy. The other layer of withheld information...

If she managed to persuade him to join the company, he would eventually learn about her baby. Although it wasn't like she expected them to be a long-term couple. She wasn't looking for that. She had plans. Goals for her career, goals for her family and, more important, goals for her life with her child. Royce didn't fit into those plans. He wasn't her type, when it came to relationships, and she was fairly certain she wasn't his type, either.

But they were attracted to each other. That was clear in the deep eye contact, the way his hand grazed her skin. And her days for having a no-strings fling were numbered. *Casual* would take on a different meaning once she had her child. On a practical level, having a wild, torrid affair with him—right now— made complete sense.

No question about it, she did want him, so much.

She wriggled against him. "I assume this means you're sure?"

Royce angled back to look into her eyes, stroking her hair in a long sweep of his hands. "Aren't I supposed to be the responsible, honorable man asking you that question, if this is what *you* want?"

Her hair tingled all the way to the roots from the rasp of his callused touch. "Then ask me."

"Are you sure this is what you want?"

"Are you kidding me? I very much want this. And

all the evidence points to you wanting me just as much," she said. "You're quite the scientist." Eyeing him, she took in the hard panes of his chest, the way his chin raised in confidence.

"It's biology." He eyed her right back with a gaze that drank her in, launching another wave of excitement through her veins.

Anticipation swirled through her until her face heated with a flush. "Biology? I would call it chemistry."

"Ah, how right you are. Good distinction." A lopsided grin graced his lips. He reached into the bedside table and pulled out an unopened box of condoms.

Morning sunshine pushed through the snow on the glass roof, dappling them with light as she tugged at his shirt and sweatpants. His skin was impossibly warm, the hard muscle shifting under her touch while she skimmed away his clothes. The expanse of his muscled chest sprinkled with hair wasn't that of a sedentary man. His sinewy planes spoke of activity, of a love of the outdoors.

She wanted to feel him, all of him, against her. Inside her. She'd never been so hot, so hungry, for any man. She reveled in the graze of his fingers as he bunched and swept aside her silk thermal shirt, sliding around the strap of the simple cotton bra she'd never planned on anyone else seeing. His avid gaze practically sizzled the fabric away. Her breasts beaded to aching points by the time he freed her. She shivered as he scraped down the thermal and underwear, until at last they were skin to skin.

The warmth of him, pressing flesh to flesh as he kissed her, ramped up her need—higher, hotter. He skimmed his mouth to the curve of her neck and she caught a glimpse of the heat in his eyes as he stroked her with his gaze. She felt it as tangibly as his caress along her breasts. Then he moved lower, kissing the inside of her thigh, then the core of her. Circling, plucking. Teasing a tingling flame higher and hotter until her hands gripped into fists.

"You're absolutely…gorgeous. But you have to already know that."

His intuitive touch made her feel like a schoolgirl. Carefree. The reality of who they were and why she had concocted a scheme to meet him seemed to fade away, melt like sun-soaked snow.

They were just man and woman, caught up in a feverish attraction. She'd had no idea how powerful that could be.

"You're making me blush."

Royce planted slow, deliberate kisses on her collarbone. "That sounds like an invitation to make you blush all over."

Oh. My.

Breath seemed impossible as he pressed against her. Still, somehow she managed to whisper, "As long as turnabout is fair play."

"Yes, ma'am." His confident chuckle heated her

flesh and he angled up to graze his mouth along her ear, her jaw.

"And by the way?"

"Yeah?"

"You're too chatty." She nipped his bottom lip.

His slow, sexy smile gave her an instant's warning before his mouth closed over her breast, one then the other until the tingles gathered force within her to a tight urgency.

She grabbed for the box of condoms and wrenched it open, fumbling to tear into a packet. He reached for her hand but she nudged him aside. Wanting, needing to explore him. She sheathed him and his groan of pleasure brought an answering groan from her.

"Naomi, there are so many more ways I want to touch you, to—"

She pressed her finger to his lips. "And you can. We will. Right now, though—"

She didn't have to finish the thought. He slid inside her, filling her as her legs glided up and around his hips, her ankles locking. In synch, they moved. She didn't know how to explain the strength of sensations already swelling inside her, the way his caresses ignited her, knew her so instinctively. Being with him was insane and somehow so damn right all at the same time.

Passion built and she felt that flush inching over her, all over, the rise of impending completion. So soon. And as much as she wanted to hold it back, she also thought of the next time, and there would be one. How much more they would share here. To-gether. For however long the storm lasted.

Just when she thought she couldn't bear the wait any longer, his hand slid between them and teased her the rest of the way over the edge. The stars sparked behind her eyelids like the northern lights splashing streaks of color across the sky's palette in a van Gogh–esque magnificence.

She savored the moment and sensations in a slow return to reality. Flames crackled in the fireplace, adding a hazy glow and the scent of wood smoke to the one-room space.

One room.

In the middle of nowhere.

Total escape.

And as she looked into his eyes, she saw he was every bit as close and, yes, as flushed with need. Her release rippled through her in rays of heat and bliss just as his ragged shout of completion mingled with hers.

His arms wrapped around her as he rolled to his side, cradling her to him. She buried her face against his chest, breathing in the salty scent of him, listen-ing to his racing heart. Trying to take in the intensity of what had just happened, so much so soon.

Her family was depending on her to persuade Royce to join their company or at least share his re-search. Most important, they absolutely did not want to alienate him and risk his going to the competition, especially now when they were trying so hard to woo major investors like Birch Montoya.

And yet, she was here indulging in a reckless passion, living up to the party girl reputation she'd never earned when she should be focused on her family's business and her baby's future.

Rolling to her back, she stared up at the snow piling on the roof, listening to Royce's even breathing beside her. He was awake though, like her, which gave her a little while longer to relish this moment.

But soon, too soon, she would have to check in with her sister again and, even more daunting, return to reality.


Delaney wasn't sure how much longer she could keep her affair a secret. She'd built her career—her entire values system—on improving the environment for generations to come. Her sister Naomi had nearly died of cancer, and watching helplessly as she'd suffered had left its mark on Delaney. Her crusade for a cleaner environment was personal. Deeply so.

Being part of an oil family dynasty made her stance tough enough, but she liked to think she brought balance to the business. Besides, the oil tycoons she knew were relatives. She loved them. When it came to friendships and romance, she opted to spend time with people who shared her common interests and causes.

Until now.

Until Birch Montoya—a man with his eye on profits more than on the survival of an ecosystem.

Although, right now, he had his eyes firmly on her, and Delaney didn't want to resist.

She leaned across the desk, her breasts sensitive with arousal along the lace of her bra as she stared at her secret lover in his fitted boxers. She'd given up trying to understand how they could argue—how they could be such total opposites—and be so turned on at the same time.

But that's how it had been between them since they'd sparred in a board meeting and ended up in a broom closet. Tearing each other's clothes off.

Like they'd done the second he'd arrived tonight. As if she hadn't known that delivering paperwork was just an excuse. An excuse that had barely held until she locked the library door behind them. An hour later they'd finally turned their attention to work in the book-lined room, fire blazing in the large stone hearth.

Work was always better in their underwear. The view made them less likely to fight about how he wanted to chew up the environment to add to the bottom line. If she thought about his ecological stance, her head would explode and their evening alone would be wrecked.

How could she want him so much and disagree with him on everything at the same time?

Her eyes were drawn to his thick dark hair falling over his forehead, his high cheekbones from his

Native American heritage. All of him handsome and brilliant and, yes, infuriating.

Birch pushed aside an architectural schematic and clasped her hand. "If the company goes bankrupt from your *requests*—" he kissed her wrist, punctuating each word "—then you'll have nothing left to win at all."

Her head lolled back at the sensations spiraling through her as he kissed and nipped. "And don't you want to be on the cutting edge of innovation in the oil world?"

"We have Royce Miller for that." Birch glanced up at her, his dark eyes meeting hers, smoldering.

"He's a scientist." Delaney tried to find her logical side, but each word came out breathy, her blood turning to liquid fire in her veins. "I'm an activist. It's different."

Birch muttered, "Tell him that."

"What?"

"Nothing." He stepped around to her side of the desk, scooped her up in his arms and sat in the massive office chair, settling her into his lap. "My point is, with Royce on board, we're already ahead of the race with other companies in being eco-friendly. Good luck getting Johnson Oil on your side if Alaska Oil Barons goes under."

"Dad's company is not going under," she retorted automatically, her legs tingling from the bristle of Birch's bare thighs.

"It's not solely your father's company anymore."

"Thanks for the reminder." She tapped the platinum wolf charm Birch had given her. She'd been touched that he seemed to know her preferences and how she avoided diamonds unless she knew exactly how they had been mined.

He'd been a welcome distraction.

The past few months had been stressful as hell since her brother Broderick and his fiancée, Glenna, had walked in on their business rival parents in the shower together, in Jeannie's office bathroom, no less. Their whole world had been upended with the Steele patriarch and Mikkelson matriarch laying down the law. They were merging their two companies and their offspring needed to get on board or move on.

So much change. So fast.

But now, Birch leaned forward, his mouth covering hers, scattering her thoughts and sending her body into motion. She swung her legs around to straddle his lap and wrapped her arms around his neck, scooting forward, which brought the core of her deliciously against the hot length of him.

Yes, she needed this diversion in her life. She needed him.

A growl rumbled in his chest. "I want you so damn much I could barely keep my hands off you in there."

"I wanted to tear your clothes off with my teeth." She nibbled at his bottom lip for emphasis, then flicked her tongue along it to trace away any sting.

"Your teeth?" He narrowed his eyes, envisioning. Fantasizing. Liking.

Just the feel of his dark eyes on her body made her breathless. Needy.

She laughed, kissing her way down his chest. "I'll be happy to show you."

"Save the thought for when we can linger." He tucked a knuckle under her chin and guided her face back up and tasted her, once, twice. "Next time you're at my place, we can play that out. In detail." He cupped her breasts, his thumbs stroking over each pebbling peak.

Desire sizzled over her skin, driving her need higher. Had she ever wanted anyone the way she wanted Birch? The way she craved him?

"Fair enough," she purred. "Can you hurry up though, so I don't finish before you're even inside me?"

"Why do you have to be so hot?" he asked, his mouth skimming along her jawline.

"Why do you have to be so insatiable?" she teased back, even as she knew their differences would one day drive them apart.

"I *definitely* don't want to fight with you." A smile creased his handsome face, his mouth brushing hers.

She forced aside worries to focus on the heat. The want. The undeniable need. "I agree one hundred percent with you on that."

In all the ways Royce had calculated and planned this solitary research excursion into the remote wilderness of Alaska, he had never accounted for this variable.

How could he have ever anticipated a research distraction like Naomi?

It was one thing to be led astray with faulty formulas—quite another to be distracted by a dark-haired beautiful woman with chocolate-brown eyes.

Royce sprawled beside her, his sweatpants a minimal barrier between his knee and her leg as she settled back into bed. She'd made a phone call in the bathroom to reassure the outside world she was here safe and sound. He gave a brief thought to her insistence on making the call privately, but then who was he to cast stones? A recluse by nature, he enjoyed his privacy too.

Although right now, he had his sights set on enjoying Naomi. The bed captured enough warmth to justify his half-clothed state. He thumbed the edge of the square plate settled on his lap and took a moment to soak in the vision of her again.

Her damp hair was piled on top of her head in a ponytail tied into a loose knot. His sweatshirt hung off her slender body, allowing a glimpse of her bare shoulder. She too sat cross-legged on the bed, plate balanced on her bare knees and thighs. They'd puttered around the kitchen for food, him piling on cold cuts while she surprised him by choosing a peanut butter and jam sandwich for herself.

For a moment, as he bit into his sub, the last few hours replayed in his head. How they had made love not once, but twice in the bed. And then another time in the shower. How in tune their lovemaking had been.

Tessie let out a hefty sigh. The giant Saint Bernard was a terribly vocal sleeper. The dog had wandered back to join them after Royce had brought the sandwiches from the kitchen area. The intensity of his and Naomi's passion had left them both hungry and tired.

The power of what they had shared rocked Royce's carefully calculated world. That level of connection was something he hadn't felt in years. But as intrigued as he was by what they'd shared, he knew he needed more information about her. Hell, he didn't even know his mystery woman's last name. He was missing something. And as much as he wanted to continue in this sexual bliss, he needed some answers.

She traced his mouth, his head tipped to the side as she eyed him. "I should have known that bear was a sign."

"What do you mean?" He struggled to follow her meaning, given her touch was distracting as hell.

"My maternal grandmother was Inuit, and she made a point of sharing mythology as bedtime stories."

"And what do bears have to do with that?"

Sighing, she settled back. "Supposedly, in our dreams, we're able to go places we would normally only experience in the afterlife. And certain themes have common interpretations."

"Like bears?"

"Exactly. The polar bear can signify a number of things, from purity to death, rebirth—or even sexual overtones." She bit into her sandwich, jam oozing out of the side. She flicked it with her tongue, winking at him.

Laughing, he reached for his sub. "What about grizzly bears?"

"I'm not sure. I'm going with a loose interpretation here." She licked a smudge of blackberry jam off her lip. "Thank goodness we didn't see a weasel."

"What would that have meant?"

"Trouble."

"Be wary if I have a dream about weasels. Got it."

"Royce, I have to know." Naomi set her sandwich down on the square gray plate. She looked at him sidelong. "Is there a femme fatale girlfriend due to show up here and fillet me for being around her man?"

"Around her man" was an interesting way to describe the last few hours. "Are you asking me if I'm single?"

"That's what I said." She picked the PBJ back up and bit into it.

"Not quite. 'Are you single' is three words. Your convoluted question was more like nineteen words that included someone getting cooked over the fire."

Chewing, she seemed to carefully consider his words. After swallowing, she shook her head. "I said filleted. That could have been sushi-style, you know." She winked at him, and a genuine smile revealed her straight teeth. "My mother was half-Inuit. I'm quite handy with a seal knife, just in case you have some vengeful girlfriend looming on the horizon."

"I'm single or I would have never propositioned you. No lurking girlfriends. Just an ex-fiancée who is now happily married to another guy." But he didn't want to think about Carrie Lynn.

"Ah, okay." Naomi shrugged and then leaned against him to whisper in his ear, "Me too. About the single part, not about the broken engagement."

Her nearness set him on edge again and he ached to kiss her, to pull her in close and feel those subtle curves against his chest, coax a husky moan from her throat. But he still needed more information before he'd allow himself to do that again.

"And we're snowed in here together."

Naomi set the sandwich back down, scooting around to face him on the bed. "How long do you plan to stay after the storm passes?"

"I'm not sure. Depends on when I finish my work. This was meant to be a retreat."

She nodded, playing with the plate edge, eyes downcast. "Your research."

Damn. There was something larger at play here. He angled his head and studied her eyes, or rather the way she avoided his gaze. "You know who I am. What I do. More than what I've told you."

She picked at a ragged bread edge on her sandwich. "What makes you say that?"

In another effort not to engage with him, she brought the sandwich to her full lips, took another bite.

Setting the plate to the side, he let out a long sigh. "I'm a smart man. That's not ego talking, a mere fact of a genetic lottery. Still, it took me a while to put the pieces together because you're such an incredible distraction. And you're good at dodging answers. Like now. You're not denying outright that you know me. You brought me the supplies, so you knew where you were going. But it's more than that."

She picked at the crust, making a veritable snowdrift of torn bread. "I do know who you are. Royce Miller, wizard of the pipeline upgrades."

"And you know this how?" His heartbeat quickened, waiting for the mystery to unravel, the pieces to fall into place.

She lifted one shoulder, wincing. "I heard you lecture once."

She had asked him more than once about his job and never let on that she knew he was a professor when he told her.

"And that's all?"

She finally fully met his gaze, those chocolate-brown eyes sharp, honed. Determined and brazen. Too much for a delivery person. "What a curious question."

"Curious that you're dodging the answer. Again.

You're not a delivery person. You sound more like a lawyer— Ah, hell, you *are* a lawyer."

He couldn't miss the confirmation in how Naomi braced her shoulders defensively.

"Wow, Royce, once you figure something out, you're on a roll."

"My question would be, what's a lawyer doing pretending to deliver goods for a friend?" Synapses firing, he pressed on.

"I didn't pretend." She gestured to the plate of food, to the pantry and the two boxes still stacked by the counter, all a result of her so-called delivery.

"You're quibbling."

"And you're a difficult man to meet."

He met research colleagues frequently. Corporations, on the other hand, seldom could get ahold of him. Which could only mean one thing. A chill coiled in his gut. "You're with an oil company."

She nodded slowly.

"No." A feeling he couldn't quite name—betrayal, maybe—gnawed at him. Of course. Was this just a new, base tactic in the bid for his brain?

The thought rocked him, causing him to reevaluate that connection between them.

She touched his arm lightly, warily. "At least listen to me, please."

The pleading in her voice might be a nice rhetorical strategy in the courtroom, but it would not sway him now. He shut down his emotions. He couldn't afford to be swayed now that he knew what this was about. Cold disappointment weighed on him that Naomi could be so calculating.

His logical side powered to the fore. "I'm not signing my life away."

"We have so many different ways this could work."

"'We' who?"

"You haven't figured that out?"

His patience for guessing had been replaced with a demand for answers. This same feeling—the one guiding his speech right now—was what made him a brilliant researcher. He pushed. "Enlighten me."

He could see the wheels of her mind churning, could almost hear the rustle of thoughts battling in her head. And he knew, this was about more than listening to some lecture he'd given.

She'd played him. And he'd been too attracted to her to see it.

"Okay," she said, her cheeks puffing with an exhale. She thrust out her hand. "I'm Naomi Steele, officially representing the newly formed Alaska Oil Barons, Inc."

# Five

So much for her no-strings affair with Royce.

The horror on his face after her announcement spoke volumes. But she couldn't outright lie to him. She'd already been fibbing by omission. That lawyer brain of hers could only justify quibbling so far.

Sleeping with him had been impulsive and, in hindsight, had actually jeopardized her chances of bringing him into the company.

Except something crazy had happened inside her since she'd met him. Business had become more and more difficult to consider. She could only think of him.

And now she'd made a huge mess of things. The happy endorphins buzzing through her after the incredible sex began to fade.

"I assume from the horrified look on your face that you heard me and you're not happy with who I am."

The need to check in on him—to make sure she hadn't dealt something like a killing blow—overwhelmed her. A tinge of guilt pushed at her, knotting in her stomach. Her instinct was to touch him, to reach out. But based on the way pain and shock twisted his dark, handsome features, she wasn't sure if her touch would be welcomed. So, she sat there on the bed and reached for the oversize comfort of Tessie instead.

The Saint Bernard woke up at Naomi's gentle scratch. Blinking, Tessie looked back and forth between Naomi and Royce. As if she understood the full depth—and unease—of the space and words between the humans, she slunk off the bed, landing on the ground with a decided thunk. The dog knew trouble was coming as surely as Naomi did.

"Let's just say, Naomi, that I'm…confused." Scrubbing his stubbled jaw with one hand, Royce leaned forward. Dark eyes trying to read and extract something from her.

He was still talking to her. He hadn't completely shut down. Not that there was a place to retreat from each other in this igloo. But he could ice her out and ignore her. The fact that he was still talking gave her hope.

"By what, exactly?"

She watched Tessie circle five times before plopping down on the bearskin rug in front of the crackling fire. The orange flames cast warm light on the dog's shaggy fur.

The rugged domestic scene was idyllic actually. So long as the tension between Naomi and Royce was ignored. The tension she'd introduced so soon after their lovemaking. But ignoring the reason she was there wasn't an option anymore.

And ignoring it wouldn't be fair to him, she'd realized somewhere during the conversation over sandwiches. When she'd made her grand plan to deliver the supplies and convince him to work for the company, she hadn't known anything about him that wasn't on his official bio. But Royce was so much more than a sharp mind or a valued corporate asset. He was a warmhearted man with protective instincts too strong to let a woman fend off a bear alone. He was an intriguing mixture of the methodical and the spontaneous, a science-loving genius with a wild streak all his own.

"Royce? Confused by what?" she asked again, wondering if he would just refuse to answer.

"What the hell are you doing here? I assume since you're a Steele, you don't need to moonlight as a delivery gal."

"I wanted to meet you. Your work is fascinating to me. I did attend one of your lectures, but you have to admit, you're tough to find for chitchat."

"Yet you managed."

"I'm resourceful?" She paused. "You're not smiling."

"What we did here this afternoon? Not chitchatting." He looked down at her bare legs.

His attention and vague accusation left her feeling exposed. No—overexposed. She wrapped her arms around her waist, his sweatshirt enveloping her body like a hug.

"Yes, well, this chemistry caught me by surprise." She raised a hand to stop him from talking. "And I swear, if you dare accuse me of sleeping with you for ulterior motives, I will seriously hurt you."

"It wouldn't be an unreasonable assumption."

"Actually, it would be a very unreasonable conclusion. My sleeping with you was a bad idea because it was a surefire way to make you suspicious or turn you against me once you found out who I am. I'm a lawyer—I should have been more logical."

"A lawyer. You're *that* one of the Steele family?"

She bristled at the way the description—the accusation—rolled off his tongue. "Yes, I'm *that* one."

In that normally unemotional, unreadable face, Naomi saw a twisting of anger glimmering in those rich brown eyes. His mouth closed tight as if containing harsh words. There was more though. The way he exhaled heavily through his nose, the way he continued to examine her like a witness on the stand… Naomi, who knew how to read people as well as she knew the law, could feel a hint of something within him that looked like frustrated disillusionment. Her meal grew heavy in her stomach, the joy of the day fading.

The buzzer for the dryer echoed in the small room. Tessie's ears twitched, and then she swung her head around to look at the dryer before chuffing in vague annoyance at being woken again. Truth be told, Naomi sent up a silent thank-you, eagerly exiting the bed to reach for her now-warm clothes. The small distraction might just give her a much-needed moment to regroup.

Still stunned, Royce didn't move from the bed when Naomi walked toward the compact stacked washer and dryer tucked away in the closet. Actually, *stunned* didn't even cover it.

He studied her, attempting to decipher the intentions of their afternoon burning up the sheets. A helluva introduction. Naomi pulled her clothes from the dryer, but seemed to linger a moment more than necessary at the machine.

A flare of anger rose in his chest. Threatened to bubble to the surface.

Most of all because being with Naomi had been good, damn good. There'd been an instantaneous chemistry there, more powerful than anything he'd experienced with any other woman. And yeah, he wanted to find some way through this mess and back to that.

For now, though, he would execute the most logical plan possible. Which involved putting on clothes.

Attempting to shut down the physical connection between them.

Hoisting himself off the mattress, he rummaged in the drawers under the bed, digging for clothes. The house's space-saving drawers and its overall functional economy had appealed to him—like everything else in this utilitarian space. Because there was no waste. No BS.

Until, of course, Naomi arrived. Then the BS factor exploded exponentially.

Pulling out a long-sleeved T, he dared to add another sentence to the now-uncomfortable quiet. A sentence to gain clarity. "Tell me why you're here."

Glancing at her, he watched as she slipped into her panties, the slight flex of her slender legs pushing the reality of their situation to the corners of his mind.

That connection—it still rocked through him. But that was a distraction he couldn't afford. "Well, Naomi? Use your words, please. You've been damn well pushing me to use mine ever since you strolled in here."

"Fine. I'm here to convince you to work for my family's company." Naomi placed her hands on her hips, standing in nothing but her panties and a gray shirt.

Damn. Damn. Damn.

"And that's it?" he pushed, shelving his attraction for the moment, knowing a moment was likely all the restraint he would be able to muster with her in the same room. "That's all you're hiding?"

"Isn't that enough?" A tinge of regret deepened her words.

He stared at her silently. Waiting. Needing... more? Of what, he wasn't sure. She messed with his mind in a major way.

Naomi stepped into her silver-studded jeans and shimmied them up, her dark hair falling out of her loose ponytail. "And yes, we want you in the company because of your research. Don't you want to see it used by a company that cares?"

Working with an ethical company—one that gave a damn—was the end goal. But he would never, ever release his work until it was fully developed. And even then, he wanted to be involved. "I want to make sure it's ready to be used. And I want control of it. So do you just want the research, not me?"

Naomi sighed, pink lips parting. "Of course we want you, because research is always going to be evolving and you're the best. But...if you're not interested in working for a company, then yes, we would settle for an exclusive on what you've developed."

He tugged on his shirt, one arm through the sleeves at a time, processing everything she'd said—and what she hadn't. "And you haven't been here trying to gain access to that?"

"I'll be honest. If it fell under my nose, I wouldn't look away."

The hits just kept coming. "Why are you going to such extremes?"

At least she'd shared her actual intentions. A

strange sort of victory, considering everything up until now had been lies. Well not lies exactly, but half-truths.

"Seriously, Royce? Your work is that good." She looked at him through long, sooty lashes.

The fact that they both were fully dressed now evened out this conversation.

"Nice try." He shook his head. "There's something else going on here. I'll ask again, and keep in mind how precarious my mood is right now, what made you go to such extremes to meet me?"

She paused for so long he thought she might not answer.

Naomi sank to sit on the floor next to Tessie and stroked the dog. "I had leukemia as a teenager."

A stab of surprise hit him. When he'd been growing up, a kid in his elementary class had gone through chemo and radiation. Memories of that coupled with the thought of Naomi being that sick… Damn. "I'm so very sorry you went through that, especially so young. And I'm glad you are sitting here today clearly glowing with health."

Naomi leaned into the Saint Bernard. Tessie lazily licked her right hand, clearly enjoying the attention—perhaps offering her own endorsement. "You're the first person who ever put that positive spin on things. They usually focus on the sympathy."

"You survived." He knelt beside her. "That couldn't have been easy."

"A lot of people don't. I had great medical care

and was also lucky it was caught early. But yes, it was rough."

Her throat bobbed, suppressing emotions—and memories, no doubt.

Royce attempted to find the thread that brought this all together. But cause and effect with people was a lot harder to discern than with scientific research. "I'm still not making the connection. What does that have to do with you being here?"

"The toughest part was my dad."

"What do you mean?" He reached out to pet Tessie, aware of the way Naomi's hand shied away from his.

"My sister and mom died in a plane crash, so he'd already lost one child. I was so scared of what would happen to him if he lost another."

"That was quite a burden for you to carry so young. And what a time not to have your mother." His parents had been a bedrock of support for him growing up. He couldn't help but think about how his ex-fiancée lost her way when her dad died.

"You're intuitive for a man."

"I think that's supposed to be a compliment."

"It is."

"I'm only drawing logical conclusions."

"Not everyone makes those connections. And yeah, I needed my mother so much then. My grandmother was around and she was great…" She shook her head. "I'm here. And trust me, I was pampered to pieces…still am."

"It's reasonable that your family would be even more protective after so much loss."

"I guess what I'm trying to say is I am a strong person. I can't take being smothered. I need to be valued for who I am and the work I do, like my siblings. I'm a lawyer. I graduated magna cum laude. And somehow, it's never dawned on my father that I could play a major role in the company beyond litigating legal issues. I know he loves me and that I'm not a replacement for my sister who died, but somehow our relationship got stuck in those teenage years. It's like if he can freeze me at that age, he can keep a piece of her alive…" She pinched the bridge of her nose, clearly holding back tears.

A slow understanding dawned on him as he made the connections. Understanding the broader implications of what she said. In a softer voice, he continued, "And that's why you're here."

She nodded slowly. "Well, that's why I'm here at your retreat. But it's not why I'm—" she pointed to the bed "—*here*, here."

"Heard and understood." He tucked the hair that had fallen in front of her face behind her ear, the need to touch her inevitable, irresistible, like a force of nature. "You don't have to prove yourself to everyone."

"Easier said than done when people don't have faith in me. You sure could help with that if you would at least meet with the heads of Alaska Oil Barons. Just listen, no obligation. I need to prove myself. You're my key. If I can get you to give our company an exclusive on your research—"

He shook his head. "I'm not ready."

"Whatever you have for safety upgrades is already better than what's in place."

"And the time I'll lose putting those in place will be time and energy better spent getting to the answers I want. Committing too soon will cause a delay in the long run. I have my eyes on the big picture."

Tessie moved from under his hand, running to the door, emitting a slow but insistent whine. She pawed at the door, scratching against the white paint. Turning her big head back to Royce, Tessie let out a low bark.

"We can give you people—"

He shook his head, the emotional pressure too damn much. He wasn't her answer. Couldn't be her answer. He had to end this conversation. "Stop, Naomi. We're done talking. I'm taking Tessie outside." He shot to his feet and closed the distance between himself and the door. He pulled on his boots and grabbed his jacket. Maybe for the first time ever, he was thankful to head out in blizzard-like conditions.

Royce's sudden move to the door set Naomi into motion. She sprang up from where she'd been seated. Practically tripped over her own two feet as she too made her way to the door. Stuffing her feet into her fluffy lined boots and shoving her arms into the pink parka's sleeves, she readied herself for the freeze-out—both from the Alaskan wilderness and from Royce.

She couldn't just leave things this way between them. She'd mishandled the situation and she needed to do her best to set things right.

Making her way out the door, she put her suddenly cold fingers into the gloves that she'd stuffed into her parka's pocket.

She was surprised he hadn't evicted her altogether, or at the very least banished her to sleep in the bathtub. She was mad at herself over the way she'd handled this, the way she'd lost control.

How frustratingly ironic that in working to be taken seriously, she'd done the most reckless thing she'd done since she was sixteen and snuck out of the house to joyride with friends after curfew the day she'd received her license. Not because she hadn't been allowed to take the SUV if she'd asked. But because she wanted to prove she was invincible. Naomi had wound up spinning out and driving into a snowbank that day—and she never forgot the anger in her father's face when he arrived on scene, reminding her of how many lives she'd put at risk.

And how many people would be hurt if something happened to her.

Since then, she'd cultivated the image of being a party girl—in appearance more than reality. Sure, she enjoyed flaunting convention, but she actually preferred her confrontations and emotional drama be contained to the courtroom.

Snatching up his gloves, she made her way to him and Tessie. Snow collected on his shoulders. A lot of snow for the relatively short amount of time he'd been out there.

Twenty feet between them, but it might as well have been half the globe. As her boots sunk into drifts, she accepted the possibility that maybe he wouldn't work with her because he believed the sex between them was motivated by business. The thought sickened her. Naomi didn't want to disappoint her family, but she also didn't want Royce to think she'd use their lovemaking as a strange kind of leverage.

Taking a steadying breath of ice-cold air, she felt awake, at home and grounded. Ready to try to talk to him, to make him understand the stakes of her offer and her attraction to him were not one and the same. Tall trees cast her snow-crunched walk in shadow. Glancing behind her shoulder, she looked back to the glass igloo in the clearing, appreciating the way it stood apart from the woods. The small building didn't intrude on the natural surroundings. No—the economic igloo seemed to mirror Royce's outlook. Understated yet impactful.

Turning her attention back to the path to Tessie and Royce, she let out a deep breath she hadn't re-alized she'd held. He turned, snow spilling off his

shoulders. Dark eyes met hers, and that spark of familiarity and excitement danced in her.

She gestured to his dog, currently walking in circles sniffing the ground. "Tell me about Tessie."

"Tell you what exactly?" He broke eye contact, his
gaze focused somewhere along the tree line.

"I was hoping my open-ended question would
lead you to reveal things I didn't expect." She thrust
his coat and gloves toward him.

"Open-ended questions, huh?" He pulled his
hands from his pockets and slipped on his jacket and
gloves. "Showing off those lawyer skills of yours?"

A small joke. The ease warmed her core. "Not
showing off if it didn't work. How long have you
had her?"

He held out his hand, holding it steady while
snow gathered in his gloved palm. "Since she was
a puppy. A backyard breeder got busted, and the
shelter needed to place nearly a hundred puppies, all
different kinds. The little breed ones went fast, but
it was tougher to place the larger dogs. Tessie also
had a broken back leg. So, I picked her and headed
straight for a veterinarian's office. She spent her
first six weeks of 'freedom' wearing a cast. Luckily
though, she healed up just fine. No lingering effects."

She smiled and, yes, her cheeks were already
starting to sting from the blustering cold wind, but
she couldn't resist the allure of his sweet story. "You
have a soft heart."

"I like dogs." He shrugged, more snow falling

from his broad shoulders. "That doesn't make me a softhearted individual. Just human."

"You've had other dogs?"

"Yes." His gloved hand clenched the collected snow into a ball that he then tossed toward Tessie.

The Saint Bernard pounced with two large paws, sending a shower of white powder poofing upward.

"Just 'yes'? I'm glad you're not on the witness stand." She knelt to pet Tessie with one hand and started gathering a snowball with the other. "I'd have to ask the judge for permission to treat the witness as hostile."

He looked at her sidelong, brow arched. "Not hostile, just guarded."

"I could have kept quiet and we would be playing in the snow, then warming up in the shower before eating supper by the fire."

"Almost makes me wish you'd kept quiet."

"We could pretend." She scooped at the snow absently. "But pretending is what got me in this position. And for that I am so very sorry. I never anticipated the powerful attraction between us. I only hoped to learn something insightful about what it would take to appeal to one of the finest minds in the field, what it would take to lure him into working for the company."

He hissed between clenched teeth. "I want to believe you."

"Then do," she said simply, and lobbed a snowball for a square hit at his chest.

"Damn. You're good at that."

"I have three brothers." Standing, Naomi took a mock bow. "I had to be good if I wanted to survive snowball fights."

"You're competitive." He stepped toward her, eyes narrowing.

"Very." The wind practically pushed her into him. Not that she put much effort into resisting.

Skidding forward a bit, she found herself pressed into his chest, his arms suddenly around her. Silence echoed between them as his eyes held hers. Heat built inside her and she saw it returned in his gaze. The cold air seemed to lose its potent punch—

A rapid succession of cell phone chimes split the air. She couldn't make herself move.

Royce patted her coat pocket. "Now your great equipment makes sense."

"That's the ringtone I use for calls from my brother. I don't have to take it if it bothers you. I realize I've thrown a lot at you today…"

"Naomi," Royce whispered, the warmth of his breath on her cheek. "Take the call."

She shook her head. "No, I'm here with you. We're talking and playing with Tessie. I'm enjoying myself and I think maybe you are too. I'm not letting a phone call mess with that."

He smiled in a slow, confident way that lit all the way up to his brown eyes. He squeezed her tighter, and she melted into his touch. Aware of nothing but the glint of promise in his eyes. The way his face moved to meet hers. A thrill tingled along her skin, so intense it was almost like flesh coming back to life after frostbite.

She would only have to move a whisper more and they would be kissing, except she needed him to make the move this time, to know that he'd found some sort of resolution to how she'd played with the truth in her reasons for coming to his cabin. Their breaths puffed white clouds in the cold air, the bursts mingling, making her ache for that connection to be real.

Royce shook his head slowly. "Ah, hell, Naomi Steele."

His arms went around her and he sealed his mouth to hers, fully and confidently. Sighing, she leaned into him, heat rekindling through her. Her thoughts about practical reasons for being here scattered like the snowflakes swirling away as she and Royce toppled backward. The warmth and weight of him was intoxicating and she wanted more, so much more—

An insistent ding sliced the air. The sound of her text messages. But she was here. In the moment. Whatever her brother needed could wait.

*Ding.*

*Ding.*

Royce elbowed up, the strong lines of his handsome face only inches away. "Someone's eager to get in touch with you. Maybe you should check."

Another *ding* echoed. The insistence was unmistakable.

She sighed in frustration. "I'll look at the messages, then turn the phone off."

Naomi, call me.

Call back. Important.

Call ASAP. Emergency.

Not something I want to text, but you need to call me. Dad had a horseback riding accident. Spinal injury.

Her whole body went numb. Except for her eyes. They burned with tears. Her father. Dread weighed her deeper into the snow, her mind filling with horrific scenarios.

As she tried to process what she'd read, a wave of nausea slammed into her, roiling hard and fast. With her tear-stained eyes, she thrust her cell at Royce and made fast tracks toward the igloo.

Not an outright run, but a lifetime of Alaskan winters gave her sure-footed steps along the icy path. Fear propelled her, along with an untimely round of pregnancy sickness.

Inside, she ripped off her parka on her way toward the bathroom, leaving a trail of gloves and boots behind as she—thank God—made it in time.

After there was nothing left and her stomach settled, she leaned against the cream-colored wall, eyes closed. Naomi set her hands over her mouth, taking a few deep breaths before forcing her eyes open.

Adjusting to the light, she blearily registered Royce in the doorway, concern in his eyes, in the way he crossed his arm. He moved toward her, sliding into the small space between her and the sink. Royce set her cell phone on the countertop, exchanging it for a washcloth. He ran the warm water, dampening it to put on her neck.

He sat next to her, leaning against the door frame. "Food poisoning?"

Weary and drained, she scrounged for the will to shrug off the question. But fear still snaked around her—fear for her father.

Staving off panic, she took a deep breath. Exhaled. Then another until she realized this was the end of the road for her games and her plans to win over the reclusive scientist.

The business just didn't seem so important, considering what had happened to her father. She'd wanted stability and, instead, what she'd gotten from the universe was even more uncertainty. An attraction so big it frightened her. A man who didn't trust her. Plans that came apart. And now her dad...

She surrendered, spilling her last secret, one she hadn't even told her family yet. "It's not food poisoning. It's pregnancy."

# Six

Stunned, Royce processed the twelve letters Naomi had spoken.

A breath tumbled out of his nose as he scrubbed a hand over his windburned cheeks. Slowly, he looked around the small bathroom. Feeling like they needed more space than an efficient bathroom like this could provide. He blinked. Once. Twice.

She buried her face back in her hands, collecting herself.

As Naomi drew in deep, measured breaths, Royce wished he could find some of that ease for himself. He was reeling.

His effort to view the situation from an objective— indeed distanced—lens proved more challenging than he cared to admit. So Royce did what came naturally. He cataloged the world around him, made sense of existing order and structures. The bright light in the stainless steel fixture drew his eyes up to the glinting white tile that surrounded them. Huge squares were arranged in a pattern on the walls, and on the cool ground beneath his fingertips.

This was the only room in the studio igloo without a full skylight. Instead, the slanted roof was kissed with stripes of glass panes. He'd never noticed that the quality of natural sunshine had a dizzying effect.

This mental exercise of grounding always left his mind refreshed, ready to tackle a difficult theoretical or mathematical problem.

Hopefully, that would also extend to this particular situation. "You're pregnant."

"Yes. Two months along. And I haven't told anyone about the baby yet. I certainly wouldn't have expected you to be the first I told." She swallowed hard, something like pain twisting in her beautiful features.

A gut punch rocked through him. She was pregnant? And the father? There was no ring on her finger and no hesitation in the way they'd slept together. Still, so many questions. He didn't want to risk upsetting her and unsettling her. She looked so pale already.

He would tread warily. In a softer voice, he began again, "Naomi."

"What?" Those dark eyes of hers, red rimmed, made her seem worn-out.

How had he not noticed her fatigue before? "I'm worried about you."

"My doctor says I'm in perfect health. Morning sickness is normal and, yes, I've been dealt a shock too."

Events from a lifetime ago scrolled through his mind. He recalled another time—when he was another person—with his former fiancée.

Carrie Lynn had been so upset after her father's funeral. The day after, she'd gotten in a car wreck on her way home from the grocery store and lost the baby. The cops had ruled it a no-fault accident, but she'd blamed herself, sunk into a depression and broken things off from him. He didn't blame her for the accident, even for a second, but he did blame himself for not being there to help her more. If he'd been driving that day, things well could have turned out differently.

Tamping down thoughts of the past to deal with the present, he took Naomi's hands in his. "It's not about your health. It's about you being careful. For your child. You went barreling off into a blizzard by yourself. Anything could have happened."

She tugged her hand back, eyes narrowing. "I don't answer to you."

So much for offering comfort. All he could do was nod. "Fair enough."

Silence passed between them. He glanced at the

counter where he'd laid her phone. Reaching forward, he grabbed it and handed the device to her.

A half smile of a thank-you. She looked down at the still-dark screen. Without looking up at him, and in a voice uncharacteristically small, she asked, "Did you read the texts?"

"I assumed you meant for me to read them since you gave me the phone rather than stuffing it back into your coat pocket."

She clutched the device. "I should call my brother."

"Yes, you should, but I need to tell you, right after I read the messages, the storm picked up. The connection is down again."

Her face scrunched with frustration, her eyes blinking fast against pooling tears. His gut knotted and he wished like hell there was something more he could do for her. He reached for her and she held up her hands fast.

"No, thank you though. I'm pretty sure if you hug me, I'll fall apart. Nothing personal. If anyone were to offer me sympathy right now, I would lose it. Hormones, probably, because I am *not* the weepy sort."

"Okay, space granted. For what it's worth, even my tech isn't getting a call through on my cell—I checked for a signal. I'm sorry. And I'm sure one of our phones will be back up soon." He took her hand. "So how about giving yourself a second to catch your breath and gather your thoughts." He stroked her wrist. "Your pulse is still too fast."

"I wish I could joke that's because of you." Naomi's grin didn't quite reach her eyes.

No, Royce could see the weight the news about her father put on her. "Me too."

Tessie nudged his back in a hello, then lay down, pressing against his side. Filling the bathroom floor to max capacity.

Naomi slumped to rest against the shower stall door. "As for being careful, I've been driving in snow since I could reach the pedals. But the storm did roll in faster and heavier than anyone expected. Not that I answer to you," she repeated.

"It's okay to be cared for."

"Cared for is one thing. Smothered is another."

"I assume you're referencing your fight against cancer as a teen."

"More like my family's reaction afterward."

A thought came to him, and normally he might not have presumed to ask, but talking seemed to help distract her, so hell, he could talk. "And it's safe for you to be pregnant? Even after having had cancer and treatments?" He held up a hand. "Not smothering. I want to know."

She lifted a shoulder, tracing the grout in the floor tile, nonchalantly. "I had eggs frozen as a teenager—"

"Hold on. Not to be invasive, but are you saying this was an in vitro?"

Her eyebrows raised. "You're asking about the father."

He shrugged. "As your bed partner a few hours ago, I am curious."

"In vitro. Anonymous sperm donor," she said clearly, succinctly. "I have no lurking boyfriends or baby daddies."

Relief, too much, rocked through him. It shouldn't matter this much to him. But it did. "And so you decided on in vitro fertilization."

"I did. Granted, I made the decision before my family changed. Before we learned about Dad and Jeannie and the merger, which has shifted the world for all of us. But I want to be a mom. I've dated some great men, but never quite The One. I have a steady career, and my health scare has always made me aware of how important it is to embrace the day. I decided to have my baby now."

"And if Mr. Right comes along?"

"If he can't love my child, then he's not Mr. Right."

"Fair enough," he said, the subject of children making him itch between the shoulder blades. The shadowy image of a lost baby he had never seen still haunted his dreams some nights. He knew that loss would follow him always. But this wasn't about him. This was about her, and a grief no one should have to endure. And to face it so young? "You were talking about having cancer as a teen. I'm sorry to have interrupted you."

She thrust her hands in her hair, scraping it back. "It was such a surreal time, wanting to hope for the future but feeling like time was running out. When you're a teen, the future is getting invited to the prom. But because my sister died, I felt like I had to grasp every chance to experience life I could, cancer or no. I still feel that way."

This woman. Damn. Her tenacity humbled him. To have been through so much—faced so much tragedy—and still be this strong. A helluva fighter, that was for sure. But for now, she didn't have to fight alone. Royce wanted to take charge, fix the past for her, find solutions to unsolvable problems. The jut of her chin made it clear she was a woman who fought her own battles. And he admired that in her. Still…

Unable to resist, he cupped her shoulder, hoping she would accept that much comfort at least. She swayed a hint, as if she might lean against his chest and take the solace he ached to give her.

A ding sliced through the moment. Naomi looked down at her phone in disbelief. The signal meant a break in the storm. She nibbled on her bottom lip, took a steadying breath. Then, as if she was channeling all her strength, he watched her spine straighten, the composed lawyer taking over her body. "I guess that means the phone connection's back for now." She pushed to her feet. "I should call right away before we lose connectivity again."

In an instant, he watched her spring to her feet and blur past him. Angling over him and Tessie, she made her way to the living area, leaving Royce seated on the tile floor.

* * *

Curled up on the sofa, Naomi scrunched her warm toes beneath the thick chunky blanket Royce had unearthed from the closet. She clutched the cell phone, pressing it hard against her ear as if the mere pressure would ensure the connection's strength.

It had taken her three tries to get through to her brother Broderick. During that time, Royce had brought her the blanket, steaming hot chocolate and an assortment of crackers.

"How is Dad?" Was that shaky voice really hers?

"They have him immobilized until the neurosurgeon decides exactly how to proceed." Broderick's steady voice grounded her, even if the news sent her nerves skittering.

"Immobilized?" Her mind reeled, attempting to imagine a force strong enough to keep her father down for any length of time. "Neurosurgeon?"

"He broke his back…two bones in his neck, actually." The words thundered through the cell speaker, piercing her heart. Stunned silence. Broderick must have sensed her tension. His hurried reassurance came next. "But he's still able to move his arms and legs."

"He broke his neck?" The words felt foreign to her tongue, like she'd been tasting a strange reality. Her eyes sought Royce across the room, craving that connection. Damn it, how had she let herself lean on him already?

"He cracked the top two vertebrae, the C1 and C2.

Actually, the C2 has a peg on it that goes through the C1. That peg is broken. Right now, there's no nerve impingement and he's able to move his legs."

She tried to call to mind anatomy textbooks to envision what Broderick was talking about a diagram of her strong father's frame inside a force of personality that had always been indomitable.

Broderick's textured and overwhelmed sigh filled the speaker. "But he has to stay in bed, in a brace. He can't move his head and, God knows, he can't fall. And he must—" his voice cracked for the first time, and then he cleared his throat "—he must survive through surgery. It's risky, but there's no choice."

Naomi absently reached for the hot cocoa on the end table, needing the feeling of warmth, of something, as she turned over her brother's words. Better to reach for that than the appealing man across the room who had offered her the comfort she truly craved. The steam danced around her face, and she blew on the beverage, scattering the steam into the studio's air. "I can't imagine—" her own voice hitched this time, but she cleared it "—a world without Dad."

"Or a world where Dad's paralyzed."

A gut-sinking feeling anchored her to the sofa. "Did the surgeon give any more details about the surgery? How is surgery going to fix the break?"

"Apparently, there's a small screw they can put into the peg on the C2 that will hold it in place. Then he wears the neck brace for six months, but there's not as much risk as letting it heal on its own, which could take months and a halo."

"That sounds good." She grasped at the hope.

"The surgery is done so rarely, the screw isn't in stock and has to be special ordered. Most people who have this kind of break don't survive."

"Okay, scary, but also a relief he's alive." Naomi's thoughts drifted from her own anxieties to Jeannie, her father's fiancée. The former rival matriarch of another oil company. Heat found Naomi's cheeks as she recalled how resistant she and her siblings had been to the family and corporate mergers. Family feuds were meaningless right now. Jeannie had already lost a husband to a heart attack… To lose a fiancé too… "How's Jeannie?"

"She's putting on a strong front, but underneath it all, I can tell she's a mess."

"That's understandable. This type of accident is…incomprehensible. Dad's such a sure seat in the saddle. He's the last person I would have expected to have a riding accident." Her hands shaking, she sipped the hot cocoa, the sweetness giving her an unexpected boost. Throwing a glance over her shoulder, she looked to the kitchen area where Royce meticulously cleaned the counter.

"They have staff with him, but we don't want him left alone. So, we've already started making out a schedule to rotate through."

"Do you think he'll allow that?" Another question—a more terrifying one—intruded on her thoughts. "God, is he even alert enough to know?"

"He's mighty clear considering the hit to the head he took. Clear enough to be frustrated, but he seems to be scared enough to be compliant." A dark laugh blasted through the cell speaker. "And honestly, he's not going to have a choice. We're as stubborn as he is. We figure we'll talk about business. He'll let us hang out as long as we want." Silence echoed through the phone. She could practically hear Broderick's gears turning as he shifted topics. "How are things up there with you?"

"Still snowed in, not sure when I'll be able to leave. I pray it's in time for Dad's surgery." She paused, weighed her options, then decided she needed to update her brother. "I, uh, decided it was best to be up-front with Royce and tell him why I'm here."

"Royce? You're on a first-name basis?"

*Brother, if you only knew.*

"We have been stuck here in a snowstorm, and for longer than I expected." She looked back at Royce, his dark features calling to her. That crackle of desire dancing along the air between them like static skipping over the rustled blanket. Excitement quickly gave way to sadness—to the reality of their situation.

"And what came of the meeting?"

Such a tricky question. She scavenged for her best lawyer voice. "We're still in discussion."

"You didn't get him to sign on at Alaska Oil Barons."

"He hasn't signed on with anyone else. And honestly, I can't think about that right now."

"You're right, of course. I guess I was just looking for a distraction."

Thank God, she'd managed to shut her brother down on the subject of Royce Miller, because she had very little chance of getting her head on straight about him with the news of her father's accident knocking the ground from under her. "I promise if there's something to announce, I'll let you know."

The day had passed in an insignificant blur for Royce as he tried like hell to control his thoughts. He didn't want to think of Naomi's pregnancy. It could too easily drag him into a pit of memories about his ex-fiancée and their lost baby. He definitely didn't want to think about Naomi's ties to her family's oil business and how that complicated their undeniable chemistry. So he concentrated on the weather.

The storm had let up in time for an Alaskan sunset. The open night sky above them—kept at bay by a layer of weatherproof glass.

From the kitchen, he'd watched Naomi sitting curled up in the thick blanket, her hair tumbling past her shoulders, framing that elegant face, making her dark eyes seem more inviting.

Since the retreat was so small, there was no way to give her privacy while she was on her phone call.

He could tell the gist of what had happened to her father by her answers and reactions. Yes, he was still angry at her, but that had taken a backseat to what she was facing with her father's accident. She had to be in hell right now, wanting to see her dad and being stuck up here.

Royce looked at her, sitting on the sofa, clutching the red mug of hot chocolate he'd given her. She absently stared forward, seeming lost in her own world. She'd spent most of the day like that, since the phone call. He'd replaced her hot chocolate twice between working on some reading material in the kitchen.

He cleared his throat. "From what I've seen via the internet, the weather is supposed to lighten up tomorrow. Hopefully it'll be clear enough for me to drive you into town."

She looked up sharply. "I can drive myself."

"I thought you wanted to spend more time persuading me to join your company." An offer to help. Damn clear she wouldn't take it outright.

She set her mug of hot chocolate down and stood up, hand on her hip. "You're the one who said I shouldn't have driven up here on my own. It's clear your 'offer' to drive me has more to do with machismo protectiveness than any inclination to hear a business pitch." Her words rolled out faster and faster, her pitch getting higher. "Which—by the way—happens to be the last thing on my mind right now—"

Her words choked off and she bit her lip. Hard. Her jaw trembled.

Protective urges churned inside him. He charged over to her and hauled her to his chest, cupping her head. A shudder rippled through her along with a near-silent sob.

He held her tightly, hoping his grip meant something. He stroked her back, smoothed her hair and couldn't help but wonder how she'd come to affect him so much in such a short time. Her pain slashed right through him. He could damn near see it flashing through his brain.

Then he realized the northern lights were beginning a path across the night sky.

"Naomi," he said softly against her hair. "Let's lie back and watch the lights through the ceiling."

As if her voice no longer could be persuaded to work, she angled back to look at him and nodded, her eyes red with worry and fatigue. She pulled off her shoes, letting them drop to the floor with a thud. Tessie stirred from in front of the fire as he took off his boots. Naomi had already started scooting up the bed. He hurried to meet her, brought her close to him as they leaned back as a unit.

Perfectly synchronized.

She laid her head on his chest, and they watched the sun wink out, exchanging the mundane orange of sunset for a crackling display of stars. Pristine for lack of light pollution. In this moment, in the quiet of it all, it was easy to forget there was anyone else in the world but them, especially as the radiant green oscillations of aurora borealis painted across the sky.

Words retreated from him. She could likely use something to distract her, something else to occupy her thoughts besides her father in his hospital bed. He couldn't find the precise thing he wanted to say to her. Every half-rehearsed formulation sounded clunky in his mind. So, he decided to share why he didn't want her to drive off alone.

With a deep sigh, he began, his head pressing down into the feather pillows. "I was engaged. She and I grew up next door to each other, both were grades ahead in school and started college early. We became friends—at first because there weren't many other seven-year-olds who wanted to talk about Pascal's calculator. In our late teens, we started dating."

He stroked her shoulder, unsure of how to proceed.

"You had a lot of history, then." She shifted, her hair dragging across his chest as she flipped to stare at the cosmic show above them. "That had to make the breakup even more difficult. May I ask what happened?"

He swallowed. Hard. Concentrated on the crackle of fire, the sound of Tessie's light snore. He found moments in the present to focus on. It'd be too damn easy to find himself stuck in the past. In those hard spaces. "The week before we were to get married, she lost the baby in a car accident after her father's funeral... She pulled away after that. And I lost her too."

"I am so sorry."

He closed his eyes, anchoring himself on the feel of the white sheets, the soft flannel texture beneath him. "She said I was emotionally unavailable when she needed me most. She wanted a partner she could count on."

"I can't claim to know everything about the situation since I've never met her, but I can say, if you knew each other for eleven years, then your reaction—whatever it was—couldn't have been a surprise to her."

"You're good at spinning things, Counselor."

"I'm just examining the facts." Naomi traced her fingertips on top of his.

And now he needed to focus on the shimmering of the overhead aurora borealis to keep himself from giving in to temptation. To resist drawing her to him for a kiss they could explore at leisure. She followed his line of vision. Out of the corner of his eyes, Royce watched a smile tug at her lips as her eyes beheld the natural light show overhead.

"Naomi, I'm trying to explain why I can't help but be protective, of you, of anyone in a similar situation. But I also want you to understand why I am the way I am, who I am."

Her fingers trailed up his arm; sincerity and empathy seemed to radiate from her touch. "We've both been through a lot in the past and it shaped who we are. I don't expect you to be anyone other than who you are. But I need for you to accept who I am."

"And you're independent."

"To a fault, yes, I am. You need to give me some breathing space."

He couldn't hold back a bark of laughter, in fact found he welcomed it right now.

"What did I say?" Her knee slid over his calf.

His body throbbed in reaction. Damn poor timing with her face still pale. "Forget it."

"Not a chance. What's so amusing?"

"You promise you won't go hormonal on me?"

She lifted an eyebrow. "Seriously? Did you just say that?"

He held up his hands. "Never mind."

"I can't decide if you're trying to be funny or if you're serious. Either way, I want to know and I will keep my infamous temper—which has nothing to do with hormones—in check."

"I just found it ironic that you want less attention. I've never met a woman who wanted space."

"That's stereotyping." Her lips went tight and prim, totally at odds with her sweater slipping off one shoulder.

He remembered well the taste of that creamy patch of skin. "Yes, it is. And you're anything but a stereotype."

Her mouth softened, delectably so. "I think you just complimented me."

"Maybe. But either way, you can be damn sure, you're not driving out of here alone." He'd barely survived the guilt after his fiancée's accident. He wouldn't make the same mistake with Naomi, no matter how much she wanted to call the shots.

And no sooner had the words fallen out of his mouth than her smile went tight.

"Sure," she said, inching away. "I really need to get some sleep."

While he knew he sometimes fell short on gauging the emotional component of a conversation, he could tell loud and clear she'd shut him down. He just wished he understood why.

# Seven

Naomi woke, blinked, confused for a moment about her surroundings. The warm weight of a masculine arm over her stomach grounded her, the stream of acknowledgments flooding back as an information wave.

She was with Royce. Her father was in the hospital. Careful not to wake Royce, she eased out from under his muscled arm to retrieve her cell phone from the bedside table. She thumbed the screen… and no messages, no signal.

Sighing in frustration, she smacked the phone down onto the comforter. The snow was so thick she couldn't even see the sky anymore.

She turned her head on the pillow to look at

Royce. He'd been so much calmer than she'd expected when she'd told him everything. Although it
was clear he was angry, and she'd almost certainly
blown any chance of getting him to join her family's
company, he'd still offered his compassion and protection. He'd still insisted on taking care of her. She
should have tried to talk to him more, but...

She'd just fallen asleep. Out like a light so fast.
She'd read that pregnancy would make her sleepy,
but she suspected her exhaustion had more to do with
the emotional outlay of her fears for her father and
her confrontation with Royce.

The hell of it all? She'd really enjoyed her time
with him—and the amazing sex—and she wished
she could lose herself in that now. But her fear for
her dad had her heart in a vise. Only the comfort of
Royce's arm around her, the warmth of his body beside her, kept her from bursting into tears altogether.

Tears were something she'd always had trouble
setting free, a facet of her personality forever linked
to her teenage years. To holding back her grief over
losing her mother and sister because everyone else
was hurting so much. To battling cancer and trying
to spare her father more pain.

Those circumstances grated on Naomi, made her
internalize her fear into a decisive, deadly logical
blade. It was what made her a damn good lawyer.
Fear of losing pushed her to assemble a facade of
brick in the courtroom. As a teenager facing down
the likelihood that her disease just might beat her,

she had chosen to emulate the wild abandon of her environment.

She'd done it for her family's sake, even though every fiber of her being shook test after test, treatment after treatment. For her brothers, sister and dad, she learned to bury the urge to cry or to express fear. Instead, she adopted a carefree air.

There had been one time she'd really let the reality of her treatment get to her and it had been the last time she'd given herself permission to lose her resolve in front of her family. A moment etched forever in her memory. The day her hair had started to fall out as a reaction to the chemo.

Naomi's hair had always been a point of pride—something that connected her to the mother she'd lost as a preteen. Naomi's mother had spoken of the way it shone with night—radiant, like a character in the old, oral stories her mother's grandmother had shared by firelight. So, when the first chunk of the hair her mother had brushed—and the hair so like her mom's that it had prompted a look into her mother's heritage—fell out, teenage Naomi had privately crumbled. Not out of vanity. But over yet another loss—the tie to her mother, her sister too.

Tears had burned in her eyes as she brought the lock to her father and siblings. Her sister Delaney had done her best to cheer her up, but even as a teenager, Naomi knew her condition wore heavy on them. Too much grief in one family only two years after that fatal plane crash.

She'd resented her body for putting them all through this. And she'd wanted her mother so much.

She still did.

Her hand slid over her stomach.

In her mind's eye, she imagined her unborn child. Names spoken by her mother during the stories she'd passed down danced silently on her tongue now. The love she already had for the baby steadied her, reminding her of the importance of connection. Of family. When she'd opted for in vitro, she'd had such plans for bringing up her baby here in Alaska, her big family surrounding the child with love too. She would embrace the future, have a family of her own, on her terms.

Right now, she couldn't help but wonder what it would have been like to have a man like Royce at her side when she'd decided to become a mother. Even thinking about it made her go weak on the inside.

A reaction she couldn't afford with her life in more turmoil than ever.

She'd seen the determination in his eyes when he'd said he intended to drive her into town. And the lawyer in her recognized that arguing with him on that point would be futile. She'd failed to win him over to the company, and she'd lost whatever romantic connection they'd shared. Both threatened to send her knees folding.

Once the snow eased and roads cleared, she would be spending a few awkward hours with him in an

# "4 for 4" MINI-SURVEY

We are prepared to **REWARD** you with 2 FREE books and 2 FREE gifts for completing our MINI SURVEY!

FREE
Value Over
**$20!**

You'll get...

# TWO FREE BOOKS & TWO FREE GIFTS

just for participating in our Mini Survey!

Dear Reader,

***IT'S A FACT:*** if you answer 4 quick questions, we'll send you **4 FREE REWARDS!**

I'm not kidding you. As a leading publisher of women's fiction, we value your opinions... and your time. That's why we are prepared to **reward** you handsomely for completing our mini-survey. In fact, we have 4 Free Rewards for you, including 2 free books and 2 free gifts.

As you may have guessed, that's why our mini-survey is called **"4 for 4".** Answer 4 questions and get 4 Free Rewards. It's that simple!

Thank you for participating in our survey,

*Pam Powers*

# To get your 4 FREE REWARDS:
## Complete the survey below and return the insert today to receive 2 FREE BOOKS and 2 FREE GIFTS guaranteed!

▶ DETACH AND MAIL CARD TODAY! ▶

## "*4 for 4*" MINI-SURVEY

**1** Is reading one of your favorite hobbies?
☐ YES ☐ NO

**2** Do you prefer to read instead of watch TV?
☐ YES ☐ NO

**3** Do you read newspapers and magazines?
☐ YES ☐ NO

**4** Do you enjoy trying new book series with FREE BOOKS?
☐ YES ☐ NO

**YES!** I have completed the above Mini-Survey. Please send me my 4 FREE REWARDS (worth over $20 retail). I understand that I am under no obligation to buy anything, as explained on the back of this card.

### 225/326 HDL GMYG

| | |
|---|---|
| FIRST NAME | LAST NAME |

ADDRESS

APT.#          CITY

STATE/PROV.          ZIP/POSTAL CODE

READER SERVICE—here's how it works.

Accepting your 2 free Harlequin Desire® books and 2 free gifts (gifts valued at approximately $10.00 retail) places you under no obligation to buy anything. You may keep the books and gifts and return the shipping statement marked "cancel." If you do not cancel, about a month later we'll send you 6 additional books and bill you just $4.55 each in the U.S. or $5.24 each in Canada. That is a savings of at least 13% off the cover price. It's quite a bargain! Shipping and handling is just 50¢ per book in the U.S. and 75¢ per book in Canada*. You may cancel at any time, but if you choose to continue, every month we'll send you 6 more books, which you may either purchase at the discount price plus shipping and handling or return to us and cancel your subscription. *Terms and prices subject to change without notice. Prices do not include applicable taxes. Sales tax applicable in N.Y. Canadian residents will be charged applicable taxes. Offer not valid in Quebec. Books received may not be as shown. All orders subject to approval. Credit or debit balances in a customer's account(s) may be offset by any other outstanding balance owed by or to the customer. Please allow 4 to 6 weeks for delivery. Offer available while quantities last.

▼ If offer card is missing write to: Reader Service, P.O. Box 1341, Buffalo, NY 14240-8531 or visit www.ReaderService.com ▼

BUSINESS REPLY MAIL
FIRST-CLASS MAIL    PERMIT NO. 717    BUFFALO, NY

POSTAGE WILL BE PAID BY ADDRESSEE

READER SERVICE
PO BOX 1341
BUFFALO NY 14240-8571

NO POSTAGE
NECESSARY
IF MAILED
IN THE
UNITED STATES

SUV. After that? She doubted she would ever see him again.

How was it that her brain—a legal mind that always served her well in thinking on her feet—was on total stun now? She needed a plan B. She always had one.

Except for now. Somehow, this one man had changed everything.

Royce's hands gripped the wheel of the SUV, his abacus key chain swaying. He'd surprised the hell out of himself by offering to drive Naomi to Anchorage to be with her family. They had chemistry, sure, but she was also a Steele.

And she was pregnant.

His gut went icy at the thought. Yet even as the thought chilled him, he couldn't ignore the need to see her safely home.

Despite the freezing temperature, the palms of his hands slicked with sweat as he navigated the vehicle on the still-snow-covered Alaskan back roads. The moisture had little to do with the warmth produced by the car's heated seats. No. It had everything to do with his beating chest, his concern for the beautiful woman seated next to him. He needed to get her to her father.

The storm had let up enough for them to leave. He knew better than to let this break in the weather pass them by, even if a selfish part of him wanted to return to the bed and just hold her. Be near her.

Flicking his eyes off the road to see Naomi, he watched her absently catalog the thick snowbanks and snow-drenched trees. Her head casually rested forehead to glass, the thick tangles of her hair obscuring most of her face.

She clutched her phone in her manicured hand, an exhale sending her body moving. "Uh-huh…Yes…I understand."

Her half whisper was so soft it stoked over Royce's senses. Dangerous on more than one level.

He gathered his attention back to the icy road, ahead and behind.

Glancing in his rearview mirror, he took in the lay of the land covered in the thick blanket of new snow. The roads were passable with careful speed and four-wheel drive, but he still needed to be on alert. They'd been driving for about a half hour and they'd yet to encounter another living soul. Even the wildlife seemed subdued, hidden still after nature's onslaught. Too bad that same peace was nowhere near echoed inside him.

"Okay. Okay. I just—" Naomi's voice mingled with the weather station on low that filled the spaces between her silence.

"Can I say hi to the baby?" Naomi asked, her tone lighter than a moment before.

From his peripheral vision, he saw her move her hand cautiously to her own stomach. Royce scratched a hand along his jaw. Damn, but this was all complicated.

"Hey there, princess. Auntie Naomi misses you."

The affection in her voice couldn't be missed. He thought of the child he'd lost. The life he'd almost had with his ex-fiancée. The secret Naomi was keeping from her family. His hands clenched around the steering wheel at the urge to keep her safe. To not let the past repeat itself. To put safety first.

Cricking his neck from side to side, he worked to ease his grip on the wheel before his fingers numbed. The road back to Anchorage always ramped him up, but not necessarily in a good way. Too much activity, noise, business clogged creative thought. It's why he'd chosen the rental igloo outside of Anchorage. The oscillation from chunks of ice moving in the water on one side and mountains on the other stimulated his brain, somehow helped him situate his thinking and calibrate his equations for a safer pipeline procedure.

To temper the desire for Naomi until he had her settled—and figure out what the hell to do next.

The scientific process, for all its precision, owed something to the humble power of nature. Still, that thought didn't keep him from noticing how the light refracted off the snow and illuminated Naomi's face as she readjusted her seat.

Tessie let out a long sigh from the back, refocusing his attention from his wandering thoughts to the present moment. Another glance in the rearview revealed an ecstatic Saint Bernard, one clearly excited to be out of close quarters. Tessie wagged her tail, head bobbing, taking in the rush of scenery, the layers of snow and ice that made their home so pristine and beautiful.

For the first time since they began their trek back to the city, they passed another SUV.

The sudden intrusion of other people jarred him for a moment and made him realize she'd stopped talking. Even though Naomi had been speaking on the phone to her brother, there'd been a way to feel as though this part of the world belonged to them and them alone.

Royce glanced over at her. "Any news about your father's condition?" She cradled the phone in her lap.

"The doctors are waiting for his blood pressure to stabilize before surgery. He's otherwise stable, stuck in bed in a neck brace, but awake and as clear as anyone with a major concussion can be."

"We'll arrive as soon as I can safely get there." His primary objective was a safe journey for her and her unborn child.

"I wanted to hear the surgery had already been done. That all had gone perfectly, and Dad was ready to jog down the hall."

"Jog?" His attention returned to the road as he navigated along a patch of ice. The tires skidded for a moment. For a Texas boy, Royce had learned the nuances of driving in these conditions like he learned everything else—relentless experimentation and practice.

She laughed softly, the sound an enticing curl

between them. "Maybe that was optimistic, but it sounded good when I was thinking it."

"I wish I could tell you everything's going to be fine, but life isn't always fair."

"If that's supposed to be a pep talk, you're not doing so hot." She gathered her hair into her fist and twisted a hair tie from her wrist to make a ponytail. Her diamond stud earrings caught the light.

"You would have known blind reassurance was a lie. I was going to finish by saying he has the best care possible and a reputation for being strong as an ox."

"Much better that time." She gave him a small laugh. But more important, a genuine one.

Victory pumped through him—over eliciting a simple laugh. He really needed to get his head on straight. "Good to know."

She tapped on the window glass, as if she was locating Anchorage with her fingertips. Her shoulders sunk as she leaned forward, eyes attentive on the snowy landscape. "I realize he has lots of family support. I just wish I was already there."

"Three siblings, right?"

"Four actually...four living, that is. Two older brothers, a younger sister, a younger brother...and my sister who died with my mother in the plane crash."

He gave her hand a quick squeeze. "I'd heard Jack Steele had a lot of kids, but that sure is a large family."

"Going to get even bigger now that he's marrying Jeannie Mikkelson. She's got four kids—two sons and two daughters—who have a claim to the company."

"The merged company, you mean."

She rolled her eyes. "Yes, merged. Which is easier said than done. Believe it or not, I care about preserving the way business is done, and I worry about this. There are so many ways it can go wrong. Even if we do work out our differences, if there's a dip in power and Johnson Oil United uses that to their advantage…"

"Which is why you wanted to bring me in, because you love the land and not because you're a lawyer jockeying for a stronger power play for your family in this merger."

She didn't speak for a moment, the blast of the heater and crunching ice under the tires the only sounds. He glanced over quickly.

Her lips were pressed in a tight line, the pink straining to blanched white. "It's okay to care about both. Although right now, business is the last thing on my mind."

"Are you okay? I mean, do you feel alright?"

"I'm fine," she said tightly, "but thank you for your concern. Do you have siblings?"

"Nope. Just my parents, older, I was a surprise." A surprise and an anomaly.

"Sounds…quiet. Is that why you're so quiet sometimes?"

He looked hard at the road in front of him, assessing the slight snow increase. Explaining why he was quiet was like trying to explain his DNA. "I'm an introvert. A scientist. I was always three grades ahead in school. It's who I am."

"And I brought all this mayhem to your life."

"I'm a willing participant, and I have the ability to retreat to quiet as needed." Squeezing her hand again, he hoped she could feel his urge to get her to Anchorage safely.

"We're very different."

"Yes, we are. Is that a bad thing?" It hadn't seemed like such a problem back at the retreat when they'd landed in bed together.

"Depends." Her head dipped and she seemed intent on studying his hand.

A wall of snow flurries intensified, forcing his attention back to the road. He loosened his grip from her, needing both hands on the wheel. It was time to focus on the road. To get her to safety.

In the ensuing silence, broken only by the weather station on the radio, a gentle snore from Tessie in the back. And in the pensive quiet he couldn't ignore the obvious any longer.

He didn't want to say goodbye to Naomi once they reached Anchorage.

Hospitals always made her stomach churn with apprehension. The too-white lights beat down on her, settling on her skin like an unrelenting sun. In all her years, a visit to the hospital had never been quick or easy.

Glancing right, she looked at Royce, who stood cross-armed, and she had the feeling he wasn't leaving anytime soon. When they'd stopped for gas, he'd called ahead for a place to board Tessie. She'd tried not to read too much into that beyond the fact he wasn't going to toss Naomi out at the hospital door, a place the dog wasn't welcome.

Royce was plastered to her side, one hand on her back every step of the way. As if she hadn't been walking on icy sidewalks her whole life.

Broderick leaned against the arm of an industrial-looking green couch, guardian-like over his fiancée, Glenna, who sat next to her mother, comforting Jeannie. Normally, Glenna's blond hair fell in fairy-princess waves around her shoulders. But today her hair was drawn back into a sloppy bun.

Jeannie's expression was obscured by her hands over her face. Even from here, as Royce and Naomi closed the distance from the entrance to the hospital, she could see how her father's former rival was racked with worry and grief.

They weren't the only ones there in the waiting room. In fact, the place was packed. As Naomi scanned the scene, she realized her family and the Mikkelsons—who she supposed were also family now—had taken over much of the waiting area.

Her sister Delaney paced the floor, darting around her youngest brother, Aiden. Poor Aiden. Normally he seemed so grown-up. Responsible. But today he looked like the teenager he was, lines of worry cutting into his face.

Delaney, nurturing as ever, rushed toward Royce and Naomi.

Trystan, Jeannie's youngest son, the rancher, had been standing off in the corner, but as Naomi came closer, he moved to the other side of his mother, eyes narrowed. "What's *he* doing here?"

The words dripped with a defensive, protective quality. She hadn't had much exposure to Trystan, but she knew he could be hard to handle, preferring the solitude of managing the ranch to family business.

Royce glanced quickly at her before extending his hand to Jeannie's son. An attempt to diffuse the tension, perhaps? "Royce Miller."

With a calculated, thin-lipped glance, Trystan stared at Royce. He held his head high, the longer hair over his forehead revealing something about his no-nonsense behavior. "I know who you are."

"Naomi and I were discussing pipeline business when your call came through. The weather's so bad, I drove her over," Royce offered by way of explanation.

Trystan Mikkelson leveled a surprised stare at Naomi. "You got an audience with the elusive Royce Miller? While you were working miracles, did you manage to convince Birch Montoya to invest a few million more?"

Broderick choked on a cough. Others looked skyward. Trystan wasn't known for his diplomacy. Thank heaven he wasn't the mouthpiece for his family's side of the business.

Royce put a hand on her shoulder, and she tried not to lean into his touch. "Naomi, I'm going to find coffee. I'll bring back enough for everyone."

As Royce turned away, Glenna sprung up from the green couch, wrapping her future sister-in-law in a tight hug. "I'm glad you're here because I really need to get back to the baby. Let's talk later. I'm going to head home and make sure there's food and fresh beds for everyone."

"Glenna? Broderick? Where's Marshall?" Naomi had only just registered that her middle brother wasn't here, a fact that surprised her. Marshall worked with the landholdings. Much like Trystan did for the Mikkelsons. Except Naomi suspected people found Marshall easier to deal with than the gruffer Trystan.

"Marshall is on his way. He was a few hours away doing a property survey and got held up by weather like you."

For the first time since she'd arrived, Jeannie unburied her face from her hands. Eyes tired from tears, dark circles attested to lack of sleep. The woman's clear pain tore at her.

The Mikkelson matriarch held out her hands to Naomi without standing. "Naomi, it's good to see you. Your father has been asking. He was worried about you out there driving in this weather."

The PA system echoed softly with a call for a doctor.

"I'm fine. Royce drove me." Naomi leaned over to give Jeannie an awkward hug. They were still getting to know each other and now they were in the middle of such a huge crisis.

Jeannie managed a half smile. "I have high hopes all will be well with your father." She drew in a shaky smile. "Of course, we've put a delay on any plans for the wedding until we know about possible surgeries. We need to focus on him getting well."

Naomi searched the woman's eyes, wondering at her motivations, wishing she knew her better. Was this delay something to be accepted at face value? Was Jeannie's love real? Or was it a shallow thing, more financially motivated?

Voicing those questions, however, would serve no purpose either way. So, Naomi just asked, "Can I visit my father?"

She hated having to ask at all, but Jeannie was his fiancée. It seemed the right thing to do, especially if the woman truly did love Jack. And if she ended up as a part of their family. Everything was still so... surreal. The engagement. The accident.

Her own attraction to Royce Miller.

Jeannie tapped her own chest, right over her heart. "Of course you should go see him. He will be glad to see in person that you're here safe and sound. You know how much he worries."

Naomi winced. "I do."

Jeannie gestured to a hospital room three doors away, past an orderly wheeling a patient down the hall on a stretcher. "Your father's talking to his brother now. Conrad is doing his best to reassure Jack that the business isn't going to implode."

Conrad had helped keep the company afloat when Jack had struggled with grief over losing his wife and child, but Conrad was more deeply invested in his own business these days. It was doubtful he could step in again. And there was also the concern of the Mikkelsons having to sign off on things... Definitely complicated. "I'll do my best to calm his concerns."

In five steps, she'd managed to leave the waiting room filled with a family learning how to talk to each other. Entering her father's room, she felt a strange sort of relief to see her uncle Conrad sitting next to her father. He looked at her with sympathetic eyes, although he had to be very upset, as well.

A memory flashed through her mind of her uncle sitting with her during a chemo treatment, watching some teenage show with her that he surely had no interest in, but he'd been there to support her. Her whole family had come out in full force for her. Right now, she fully realized for the first time how much it sucked to be on either side of this kind of health crisis.

Her uncle motioned for her to come closer, and Naomi made her way to where her father lay.

Oh God. She knew, logically, that her always dashing father with his dark hair and bravado would look rough. But all the imagining in the world could not prepare a child to see their once superhero-like parent so horribly broken.

A neck brace pushed her father's graying hair up, seeming to highlight the massive deep blue-and-purple bruise on his forehead, his face swollen from the trauma.

Jack Steele's eyes flicked to her, and she took in the sight of the IV in his arm, the constant data rolling across a blood pressure monitor. A heart monitor too. And some other screens she couldn't readily identify.

"Hey, baby girl." His voice still sounded strong, a small comfort. Uncle Conrad moved to the sofa in the room, giving them space.

Naomi reached out her hand to touch his, feeling like she was in a nightmare. "Hi, Daddy. I didn't mean to wake you."

"I'm not sleeping. All I do is lie in this bed, staring at the ceiling." He'd never been a good patient.

She tried to joke, looking around the room at the many flowers already taking residence around the recliner chair with the pillow and all the available counter space. "I could have sworn I heard you snoring."

"Nah, not a chance."

"Well," she said, glancing at the neat handwriting on the board that charted her father's progress and medication schedules, "the nurse has written there that you're well past the time you can have a sleeping pill."

"I hate taking meds." His gravelly voice sparked with irritation.

She understood that feeling well after having had her body pumped full of poison for months. She empathized with the frustration of being out of control, of being trapped in a broken body.

"You need to rest so you can heal. We want you as strong as possible for surgery."

"Uh-huh. If I'm in pain, I'll let you know to call the nurse." He looked at her with intense eyes, and though he couldn't move much, Jack still had a way of commanding attention.

"When have you ever admitted to pain?"

He mock-scowled. "If you're here to nag, you can go home. Call Delaney to babysit me."

"You just want her here because she's a pushover."

His laugh wheezed a bit and he stifled a wince. "You're your father's child, for sure."

"That I am. So, no underreporting pain. I'm watching your blood pressure. Your secret is out. It's the quiet indicator of your discomfort."

"Duly noted. But enough of that serious talk." His fingers moved on the bed, causing a rustle on the blinding-white sheets. "It's been a long time since we had a campout."

"Once you're better, perhaps we can institute family campouts again." She hoped. God, how she hoped.

"Sounds like a good idea."

"Mom loved those times away from everything." Her throat closed with emotion over memories of her mother. Mary had been more like Delaney, soft but with a quiet determination under it all as she'd balanced a larger-than-life husband and six children. "Looking back, I realize you both took us on those trips to give us a sense of normalcy, to teach us to be more than trust fund babies."

"And it worked," he said proudly. "You all turned out damn good. Your mother would be so pleased."

"Thank you, Daddy, it means a lot to hear you say that." She squeezed his hand. "We'll be camping by this summer. I'm certain of it."

"Jeannie's top-notch at fishing. Maybe we can plan that for after the wedding. I wish we didn't have to delay the ceremony…"

Glancing back at the door, Naomi thought of what now constituted family. And the new addition to the family that she'd yet to tell anyone about except Royce. "We'll need a caravan if we're including both sides of the family for that camping trip."

She couldn't help but wonder if he really would be able to take those trips again. Would he play with her child the way she'd dreamed? Her throat clogged with emotion and restrained tears.

"It would be a nice chance for all of you to get to

know each other better, like at the little bachelorette party you girls had at the house for Jeannie. Thank you for that."

She felt a hint guilty for the frustration she'd felt over arranging that party, the shock of her father's engagement to their business enemy still so fresh.

She nodded, looking at her father. In a choked voice, she continued, "I only want you to be happy."

"You have to know there's nothing I want more than for your mother and sister not to have been on that plane. But I can't change the past. Your mother loved us. I've never doubted that for a moment. She would want us to be happy."

"Change is difficult. And quite frankly, you couldn't have come up with a bigger way to upset the applecart." She winced the instant the words fell out of her mouth. She shouldn't be bringing that up right now. Grief must be getting the best of her even though she was supposed to be calming her father.

"Truth. But let's not talk about the accident. I can't believe I let a horse get the better of me. Not his fault. Want to make sure everyone knows that. Now let's talk about something else before my blood pressure has people overreacting," he said with a hint of teasing in his bloodshot eyes.

"Sorry about that." She kept herself positioned to lean over his bed, to stay in his line of sight. "Back to happy talk."

"Tell me about Royce Miller." Ever the businessman, even immobilized in a hospital bed.

She should have known he'd already heard about her impulsive trip.

An image of snuggling on Royce's bed watching the aurora borealis filled her mind's eyes. With her dad's blood pressure already on the rise, there was no way Naomi would be sharing details of her relationship with the sexy scientist.

# Eight

The visit to the hospital had taken everything out of Delaney.

Seeing her indomitable father laid low terrified her. She'd lost her mother. Her sister. Then there'd been Naomi's cancer scare. Delaney couldn't deal with the idea of losing her father.

But what kind of woman was she to use that fear to justify being with Birch now?

She'd broken speed limits to get here. Broken faith with her family every time she hid her relationship with him. Seeing her sister working so hard to bring Royce Miller into the company made Delaney feel all the more like a traitor to her beliefs by having an affair with Birch.

Still, she needed this. Needed him.

She snapped the band of his boxers. "You should get rid of those."

Birch trailed his fingers to the front clasp of her bra and with a deft flick, the cups parted. Air swept over her breasts, her nipples pulling tight and tingling. Every nerve hummed to life, her senses on overload, breaths full of patchouli, her gaze drowning in the whiskey hues of his eyes, luxuriating in the muscular planes of his chest. How could one body store so much heat in winter?

And she wanted more.

She tugged at his boxers, but it was tough to pull them off while she was sitting. In a smooth move, he locked his arms around her and lifted, her feet dangling just off the floor as she kissed him. Or he kissed her. She wasn't sure, but somehow their underwear landed on the plush wool rug.

Delaney slid a condom from the pack they'd set on the desk earlier when they'd had frenzied sex in front of the fireplace in his home office. She rolled the condom down the length of him, slowly. His eyebrows lifted at how very much she took her time. Angling forward, he captured her mouth, catching the moan.

Biting her bottom lip, she raised up on her knees, her breasts rubbing against his chest. His pupils widened with desire just as his eyes narrowed. A shiver of awareness rippled down her spine. She slid over him again, taking him inside her, slowly, fully.

His fingers dug into her bare hips, guiding her as he thrust, again and again as she met his rhythm, his pace. The crackles in the fireplace echoing the snaps of electricity traveling through her. Her neck arched and he covered her pulse with his mouth, hair sliding along her spine as she savored the way he knew just where…just how…to touch her.

The rasp of his late day beard was a delicious abrasion against her tender flesh. His ragged breaths heated over her skin, her gasps accelerating along with his. They were always in sync that way. Maybe some of that had to do with the hidden nature of their affair. It added an edge to their time together.

Or perhaps they were both afraid it couldn't survive the harsh light of their differences, leaving them frenzied to take all they could before this connection imploded. Every time she pondered the thought it just made her more determined to stop thinking. She wanted to feel, to savor, for as long as they could because being with him was…

Incredible.

Just the memory of their other times together was enough to send her orgasm unraveling inside her in wave after wave of bliss. Birch thrust his hands into her hair and kissed her, taking her cries of release into his mouth, his own low growls of completion mingling with hers.

Sagging against his chest while her galloping heart slowed to a trot, she breathed in the scent of him. Of them. Perspiration and sex and a musky blend unique to the two of them.

Birch swept aside her hair and stroked her back, the calluses on his fingers a sweet, sandpapery abrasion. "When are we going to stop sneaking around?"

She kept her face buried in his neck, avoiding his gaze. "Aren't you having fun?"

"You know the answer to that." He dropped a kiss on top of her head.

"Then let's just keep things the way they are."

The disappointment on his face stung her with guilt. But she flinched away from saying anything. Confrontation was not her strength. A weakness in a family full of pushy extroverts. Passive aggression was more her speed.

And she intended to keep this sexy pocket of happiness all to herself for just a little longer.

Royce's boots thudded on the hospital tile as he made his way to Naomi, careful to avoid the wettest spots on the recently mopped floor. For the past few hours, he'd parked himself in the waiting room amid the Steeles and the Mikkelsons. The tension had left him uncomfortable, but not as uncomfortable as the two merging families had seemed with each other.

He'd left and made a trip to the store, waiting to return until late enough that the hospital would have quieted, the families would have left.

A time when Naomi would be alone and perhaps need him.

All that time sitting had left him restless. Ironic, perhaps, because he'd grown accustomed to long stretches in front of a computer or whiteboard doing research and solving equations. The fundamental difference between those scenarios and this one was that he had felt productive in those instances. Like he was doing something.

He'd never suffered idleness well.

His hand closed tighter around the bag of food he'd brought, all too aware that stress had kept Naomi from taking care of herself.

As he balanced the juice and snacks in his hand, he made his way to her. He knuckle-rapped the door. From the other side, he heard the sounds of footsteps padding against the tile in a hurried fashion.

The door swung open. Damn.

Even rumpled and weary, Naomi looked beautiful. Her dark hair fell in a ponytail wave over one shoulder. She wore a hoodie with tights, a casual outfit that still hinted at her curves. Adjusting her weight from one socked foot to another, her eyes danced with something that looked like grateful relief. Seeing she was happy to have him there…that gripped him. He didn't want to think about what his reaction to her might mean.

She looked around, poking her head outside the door frame. "How did you get past the nurse's station?"

"No worries on that. I'm here. I've been in the waiting room actually. I wanted to be sure you had snacks if you're not sleeping—and you weren't."

Peering into the room to the sofa with the still perfectly folded blanket. No signs of rest.

"I can sleep tomorrow. I'm afraid to take my eyes off him."

"That's understandable." He held up his offering—cheese, crackers, juice and two slices of pizza. "I thought you might be hungry. Sorry, but the pickings are thin this time of night."

"It looks amazing, actually." She nodded toward the two simple straight chairs—wood with worn maroon cushions—left over from earlier visitors. She sat down in one, patting the seat of the other, inviting him to join her. He did, satisfied to accept a stolen moment with her.

She took the food and dug in with clear appreciation.

"You know you can call me or text me if you need anything."

She chuckled softly, swiping a cracker crumb from the corner of her mouth. "Do you realize I don't even have your phone number?"

That fact had escaped him. "Well, hell. We need to rectify that."

He fished his cell phone from his pocket, sheepishly handed it over to her. Naomi's face lit up as she entered her contact information and slid it back to him, chewing on the corner of her lip. He sent her a message—just a smile. Her cell vibrated in her pocket. Connection official.

"Thanks." She gave him a shaky smile back, then

glanced toward her father again, worry furrowing her brow. "The surgery seems eons away, every second so scary even beyond concerns of a stroke from his high blood pressure. What if he sneezes? And jerks and paralyzes himself?"

"There's nothing you could do about that one. That imagination of yours is working overtime."

"Part of my job, imagining all the possibilities so I can plan accordingly. You should understand that with your work too. It's not like we can shut down our imaginations after hours."

"True enough." He lifted her feet, started rubbing them through her socks.

She moaned softly, some of the tension easing from her face. "That feels amazing. Thank you." She popped another cracker into her mouth. "You're incredibly thoughtful."

"Is it working?"

She tipped her head to the side, her dark ponytail swishing. "What are you trying to accomplish?"

"Winning you back into my bed again once things settle out with your dad," he said simply, honestly.

"Winning me into your bed again? Did you really just say that?"

"I did." He leveled a stare her way, the spark between them intensifying with each second that passed.

"Do you really think having an affair is possible? Especially if you're working for the company?"

"Fine. Then I won't consider working for the company."

"You're considering working for the company? When did you...? Um, how did you...?" she stuttered.

Hell, he hadn't known he was considering it until the words fell out of his mouth. But admitting that would sound far too illogical. So he settled for, "I've been mulling over your offer. I still am."

"Care to share more about your...mulling?"

Sliding an arm around her shoulders, he let his thoughts shuffle and move around like puzzle pieces in search of a possible fit. "Consider this. What does it matter if we're sleeping together while I'm working with your father's company? You won't be my boss. I won't be yours. There's nothing you could say to change the results of my work. So, after hours are after hours."

"Have you thought about the fact that I'll be as big as a house in a few months?" She leaned in. "There's a baby growing in this belly."

"So I hear," he said, doing his best to hide the gut kick of those words.

"And that doesn't bother you?"

He weighed his response carefully, because yes—hell, yes—the thought of entangling his life with a baby's scared him spitless. But he wanted her that much. "I think you and I have talked enough for one night." He stroked her hair back from her face. "I'm going to leave now. You should get some rest."

To make sure she didn't have enough time to press him further, he leaned in to kiss her, and damn, the feel of her lips, the sweet stroke of her tongue, made him wonder how long he could wait before he had to see her again.

Naomi paced outside her father's door while the nurse gave him a bath. Exhaustion soaked into her bones, and the fact that she still had the ability to walk without breaking down in tears seemed like a helluva surprise. Sleep hadn't been possible in her last twenty-four hours, and the pregnancy had drained her additional stores of energy.

As much as she wanted to be present for every moment of her father's hospital stay, she knew she needed rest. If not for her sake, then for the sake of her unborn child. Soon, the next family member would come to relieve her and she could get home, crawl into bed and sleep. Hard.

Her insomnia had more to do with the late night conversation with Royce, along with the foot massage and his kiss, which tempted her to lean on him.

She heard a commanding, brusque voice echoing down the hall, pulling Naomi away from the fantasy of sleep—and questions about Royce.

Trystan Mikkelson approached, flanked by Jeannie.

He gave Naomi a curt nod as he approached. His gaze was intense, brows furrowed, everything about his body signifying distance and the need for space.

She did her best to smile at him, to feel like they were family.

The attempt was unsuccessful, judging by the way his focus returned to his mother, away from Naomi and the realities looming behind the door to her father's room.

Jeannie, normally so smoothly professional and composed, looked like she hadn't slept in weeks. She hugged her bulky sweater tighter around herself, a tissue clutched in her fist. "How did he do through the night?"

"We had a nice chat and then he slept well. His breakfast just arrived." Naomi's stomach lurched at the olfactory memory. Just another item of food that made her ill during this pregnancy. The weight of the world slammed into her a little bit more. Focus. She needed to focus. She thrust out her hand to her future stepbrother. "Trystan, hello."

Trystan's rugged exterior showed nothing of his emotional state. Probably why Charles Mikkelson Jr. had become the face of the company since his father had died. Always right there helping his mother.

Trystan tapped the brim of his Stetson. "Hello, Naomi. No offense, but you look exhausted. Mom and I have this."

Naomi had to confess, "I could do with a shower and a nap."

Jeannie touched her wrist lightly, a gesture that still came off a bit awkward and uncomfortable, given how long their families had been enemies. "How are you going to get home? You're so tired it can't be safe to be behind the wheel." She turned to her son. "Trystan, you should—"

Naomi cut her short. "Thank you, but Broderick and Glenna arranged for a driver to be on call at the hospital at all times. The car should already be downstairs waiting for me."

Jeannie smiled, looking more than a little weary herself. "Okay, then, sweetie. Take care."

Naomi reached in for a hug, half bumping into her future stepmother in the process. Damn. She anxiously awaited the moment when this sort of contact felt natural.

She waved over her shoulder at Trystan, hurrying to get to the outside of the hospital and to the Suburban Glenna had sent for her.

As she entered the backseat of the SUV, she counted her blessings for at least finding a decent connection with one Mikkelson.

The ride to the Steele compound passed in a whir of snow. Naomi practically forgot that a chauffeur was present and driving the car. His deep rasping cough called her attention out from a nebulous nowhere, plopping her down in the present, her eyes roving over her family's spread.

As a child, her home had seemed like a castle on the outskirts of Anchorage. The mansion stood on a cliff, overlooking mountains. Tall pine trees formed a protective circle around the building proper, and a slate path led from the main house to the stables. Hours were spent there as a child, among the horses. It was where freedom had first felt possible to Naomi. Even though Brea had been Marshall's twin, she had been the sister closest in age to Naomi. They'd been close. Only a year apart in age. Inseparable. Losing that connection had been—still was—devastating.

She rested her head on the cool glass window, thankful for the marked contrast from the hot nervous sweat on her nape.

Her eyes fixed on the barn, on their horses—the love of the animals her father had passed on to her and her siblings. A wince of pain shot through her as she thought of his riding accident. Such a fluke as he was so sure-seated in the saddle.

Tires crunched along the ice and the Suburban slowed to a stop in front of the main doors. She hopped out, barely two steps into the great, gray building before her sister Delaney emerged from the room adjacent to the foyer, her dark hair contrasting with the cream walls where large paintings of Alaskan brush hung.

Delaney leaned against the glass table on the farthest wall, chewing her lip. "How was Daddy?"

"Feisty as ever. The doctor's supposed to come by this afternoon to discuss a possible surgery date. We'll want to be back there by then."

"Yes, of course." Delaney drew in a shaky breath. "Just so you know what you're walking into. We have an issue that needs discussing. Just with the family. The Steele family."

The prospect of having to perform family duties at this moment seemed damn impossible. "Now? I can barely stand up, much less think."

"You have to. We need you. You're the family lawyer."

Naomi waved a hand. Dismissive. Firm. Knowing she needed sleep for the sake of not only her own sanity, but for the baby, as well. "The business has a team of lawyers—"

"Yes, but you are our lawyer, a Steele. Your opinion carries the most weight."

Family first. That old mantra churning something in her.

"Thank you," Naomi said, a faint blush dusting the apples of her cheeks.

"Just stating facts. You're a damn good attorney."

And those lawyer instincts told her that her siblings had sent Delaney with this request because she was the most mild-mannered of the bunch. But she also wasn't to be underestimated.

Naomi gestured to a nook in the foyer, the one that seemed unassuming—an oversize windowsill to the uninitiated. But this was the spot where as kids, Naomi, Brea and Delaney had snuck away to talk. It seemed appropriate now. "What is it you feel the family needs to discuss?"

"We have two issues at hand. First, Dad's clicking along well mentally now, but if things go south at any point we may need to make medical decisions for him. With all due respect to Jeannie and Dad's engagement, they're not married. So, if he's incapacitated, she has no say. Am I correct?"

True, but God, her dad would go ballistic if he knew they were having this conversation. Still, they needed to look out for his best interests and they did know him. "Legally, you are right as far as me having the power of attorney. But it will be a delicate balance. When Dad recovers, he'll raise holy hell if he thinks we shut her out."

Although, knowing they'd shut Jeannie out might just force him to recover faster. Not another soul on earth could rival her father's strong will.

"True about the power of attorney. But it's still the day-to-day stuff that worries me. As much as they may have feelings for each other, does she know his medical wishes? Does she know him that well?" Delaney asked tentatively. She'd always been more of a peacemaker, not an easy role in their family of volatile personalities.

"I have told you the law. We'll handle the diplomacy if the situation arises." She prayed it wouldn't. Shoving the thought away, Naomi found it hard to stay objective. To stay purely in the lawyer mind-set. Too raw. "Let's take one crisis at a time."

"If it needs addressing, that will fall to you."

"Why me? Why not Broderick?"

Delaney blinked at her, drawing her slender legs to her chest, looking much younger, recalling a time before life disrupted their happy family—their peace. "Your legal skills with words. Broderick's more a bull in a china shop. And in case you haven't noticed, he's been off his game from lack of sleep since Fleur's going through that bout of colic."

True. And he had Glenna to share the parenting with. Naomi touched her stomach lightly. How would she manage this on her own? Her plan had seemed so right before everything changed in her family, but now she feared coming up short for her child.

All of which she would have to worry about later. Right now, she needed to focus on her father.

"Fine." Exhausted, terrified for her father, the tight response was all she could manage.

"Broderick is busy playing host to everyone. Marshall is barking orders. Aiden's a kid. And me? I'm not pushy enough, but I'm good at patting hands."

"Okay, okay, I agreed. You said two issues. What's the other?" Naomi sighed, steeling herself. Yep. Her siblings had definitely selected subtle, gentle Delaney to win Naomi's cooperation.

"If the surgery doesn't go well and Dad's incapacitated—or worse—we need to have a plan ready to roll. We can't afford for the Mikkelsons to step into the power void. Things are all the trickier as Broderick and Glenna have started sharing the CFO responsibilities—and of course he trusts her. God, things are getting muddy. Start thinking. After we finish at the hospital, we're going to meet tonight after supper while Jeannie's with Dad and Glenna's feeding the baby."

And just like that, unrest threatened the tentative peace they'd brokered with their longtime rivals.

Before Naomi could respond, the doorbell rang.

Saved by the bell, quite literally. She leaped to her feet and peered through one of the windows flanking the door to find...

Royce.

He stood outside, snow gathering on his parka, Tessie at his heels.

# Nine

Royce had intended to go to his place and sleep. Or work. But somehow, he'd ended up here.

Even though he knew stepping into the Steele lair meant stepping away from his quiet, solitary realm of research and facts, where he worked long enough to keep nightmares about the past from haunting him, he hadn't been able to stay away. Being here, with this large and looming clan, placed him that much closer to becoming a part of their team. Being a part of other peoples' lives, people to care about.

But saying goodbye to Naomi—well—just not an option.

So here he was. With his dog. Awkward as hell. Social nuances sometimes slipped past him, his head stuck in the scientific world of black-and-white. There were so many people in this rapidly blending family, he was going to need some kind of pneumonic device to remember all their names.

Naomi bounded up to him, her dark hair swaying as she approached the archway between the hall and the great room. "What are you doing here?"

Damn, she made jeans and a lamb's-wool sweater look like runway glam. And her knee-high leather boots sent his pulse jacking upward.

"I understand you're looking for a consultant." Thank God Tessie was on her best behavior, sitting like a princess beside him.

"Now?" she whispered. "You want to talk about that *now*?"

He breathed deeply, taking a moment to stabilize his emotions. Reaffirm that coming here—to this mansion with soaring ceilings that reminded him of grand cathedrals—had not been some terrible miscalculation. In that breath, he surveyed the space, his eye catching on the great room beyond Naomi, the gathering space full of multiple sofas and seating areas large enough for such a massive family.

A blaze hungrily crackled within the gray slate fireplace. His eyes traced upward to the sprawling moose antlers mounted above.

Royce noted the way the decor pulled together sophistication with an air of a bygone time in Alaskan history. Rustic, rugged elegance. The nods to the hunt—the deep, rich colors of burgundy and brown—reminded him a bit of Texas, another place of possibilities and open land.

A blonde woman—Glenna Mikkelson, most likely—rocked a baby in a thickly padded rocking chair. She attentively cooed at the sleeping baby. A Siberian husky puppy lay over her feet, ears and eyes alert to Tessie, but staying blessedly still.

Beside the blonde, a man sprawled on the wide leather sofa but quickly stood and took hold of the husky pup's collar. Naomi's brother, no question. He stared at Royce with ill-concealed interest.

Royce shifted his focus back to Naomi. "If that's what your family wants, but that's not why I've come. I realize you're in the middle of a crisis." He held up his hand. "I brought pastries. I'm a Southern boy. My mama always said bring food."

The blonde woman slid off the rocker, rising to her feet. She carefully adjusted the infant onto her left shoulder, a smile resting easy on her face. "That's very thoughtful of you," she said. "This is the apple of Broderick's eye—our daughter, Fleur."

"She's a heart-tugger," he said simply, thinking of the child he'd lost…of Naomi's baby on the way. He'd avoided children for so long and now there was no more hiding.

Broderick thrust his hand out. "Welcome. Thank you for the pastries. We can never have too much to eat around here, especially with the whole crew in town. We appreciate you stopping by."

"No problem," Royce continued. "I'm sorry to intrude and sorry about having my dog along—"

Glenna stopped him short. "No need to apologize. I adore my Kota." She reached down to scratch the Saint Bernard's ear. "I'm glad you didn't leave—"

"Tessie," he supplied, looking down at his massive pup. The dog seemed to wink at him, a tongue lazily sliding out of her mouth into a light pant. She nuzzled his hand with her great head.

"Yes, glad you didn't leave Tessie in the car." Glenna adjusted the baby on her shoulder, rubbing a soothing hand along her back. "Thank you again for the, uh, pastries."

Thin excuse to show up. Busted. "I also wanted to make sure Naomi arrived home safely from the hospital." Another lame excuse, he knew. He could have called. For a genius, he was coming up aces in the "too obvious" department.

Naomi lifted an eyebrow. "Oh really."

"Yes, really."

A willowy, dark-haired woman stood. "I'm Delaney Steele, by the way." She raised a hand absently, a softer, quieter version of her sister. "I truly would love to chat with you, but I need to help Trystan and Jeannie."

*Delaney Steele.* The name clicked in his mind. She was a well-known conservationist crusader with a reputation for holding her family's feet to the fire on safety issues. Someone he could consider an ally if he chose to sign on.

And yes, he was seriously considering Naomi's offer, though he couldn't quite believe it of himself. Maybe Naomi's words had sunk in, about the cost of waiting too long to implement the schematics he had so far for upgrades.

"Nice to meet you, Delaney. I've read some of your blogs."

She flushed and blinked fast. "Thank you, I'm honored." Her smile faded. "But I do need to get back to my father. I know the hospital must feel overwhelmed by so many of us, but we can't imagine leaving him alone…or missing the chance to see him if…"

She swallowed hard.

Broderick gripped her shoulder and turned her to face him. "He's going to be fine. We're all here for support, not on a death watch. We're all too stubborn to let that happen. Marshall's flying in now. Uncle Conrad and Aiden have gone to the water to meet the seaplane." He glanced at Royce. "Marshall and Aiden are our brothers."

There were so many people in this family, Royce wondered if they'd ever considered keeping flyers by the door, complete with a family tree as a cheat sheet.

No sooner had the thought about the large family crossed his mind than the space cleared out with excuses of dog running and baby feeding, leaving him and Tessie alone with Naomi.

"For a family that wants to win me over as a business partner, they sure did bolt fast." He leaned in, his voice low.

She touched his arm, looking up at him between thick dark lashes. "You made it clear you're here for me. You couldn't have been any more obvious."

The spark rattled his system. Yep. Busted. "Guilty as charged." He held up the bag. "Hungry?"

"Always." Her lips parted slightly, that electricity passing between them like static on winter air.

"Should we stay here or go to the kitchen—" His eyes locked with hers.

"I have a suite here, like my own loft apartment." Naomi seemed to move even closer to him, the distance between them feeling minimal, flimsy. "Let's go there. It's a little quieter."

He gestured ahead. "Lead the way."

Anticipation and a splash of apprehension quickened Naomi's steps as she led Royce to the elevator. Peeking her head around the corner, she checked for lingering family members in the hallway.

The house, surprisingly silent for the amount of family present on the compound, seemed to aid her on her surreptitious mission. Not that, as an adult woman, she had to justify her time with Royce.

But she didn't want the complications of the questions her siblings would launch at her if they saw her inviting Royce into her private quarters. Soft steps across the dark wood floors, her hands trailing behind her, close to the rustic-inspired walls textured with paintings of the wilderness.

The heat in the elevator had nothing to do with

the temperature of the mansion, but everything to do with the heat of him radiating into her back. So close.

An indulgence.

She was allowed that.

When the door opened to her loft in the east wing of the house, her stomach somersaulted. She couldn't tell if it was nerves or from her pregnancy. Possibly both.

Naomi tried to recall the last time a man had come into this space—her sanctuary. So different from the rest of the house, which boasted old Alaskan charm. Her narrow, long loft took inspiration from her eclectic spirit.

Royce motioned for her to precede him out of the elevator, such a quiet man full of old-world manners. His hands tapped lightly along her trinkets that populated the built-in wood bookcase at the far wall of the loft, which separated her bedroom from the main living area. As if he was cataloging the knickknacks as a means of learning more about what made her tick. Certainly, the clusters of framed family photos spoke of her love of the outdoors—skiing, fishing, horseback riding.

And a cherished photo of her mother, another of her sister Brea. Those losses never stopped hurting.

That wall, past the sofa and coffee table where a smattering of photography books framed a pottery vase that had always been her favorite. Different sculptures from her travels were showcased and she found herself seeing them all through new eyes. His eyes. How surreal to have Royce in her space, in her home. So different from the stark igloo in the wilds.

Having him here, where he could see some of who she really was, made her want to know more about him.

"What does your place look like?" She knew from his file that he'd bought a condo on the outskirts of Anchorage.

"I bought it already decorated."

"Oh," she said, deflated. Not much to learn there.

"Easier than hauling a bunch of meaningless furniture from Texas. I donated the old stuff to charity."

"That was really kind of you." She was touched. Truly. But still, she wondered. "You brought nothing from Texas?"

"Actually," he said, "I did bring my vintage Pascal's calculator."

"Oh wow, that's really cool." She envisioned him traveling with that seventeenth-century treasure, placing it in his generic condo along with his Saint Bernard.

He was definitely an original.

She walked deeper into her suite. During the day, her loft didn't need any artificial light. Huge windows allowed the Alaskan sun to poke through, permeating the living area.

Their footsteps were muffled as they strode along the Inuit rugs—gifts from her grandmother when Naomi had gotten her first college apartment, another cherished touch in this space.

From the rough-hewn beam on a slanted, arched ceiling hung a crystal chandelier that sent prisms dancing on the cream-colored sofa, brightening the quarters.

Tessie bounded ahead, examining the L-shaped kitchenette around the corner. Short-lived attention to the kitchen though. As soon as Naomi opened the sliding glass door to the glass-sealed balcony, Tessie padded over on fat paws, making herself comfortable outside.

She circled three times, clearly enjoying the sun as she plopped down, rolling her back out. The dog seemed blissful.

After such an emotional night watching over her father, Naomi needed comfort, needed a distraction. She'd always prided herself on being independent, but had to confess, the way Royce had shown up at the hospital, the way he was here now with his dog and pastries—so eccentrically wonderfully himself—she was on the verge of tears.

He touched something in her soul. And as much as that scared her, it also drew her in.

He held up the bag of pastries again. "Are you hungry?"

"Yes," she said, "for you."

With a growl of approval, he tossed the bag onto the black marble table tucked in the corner of the L between her kitchen and living area.

His hands slid up to span her waist with a bold, large grip. She cupped his shoulder, ready, eager to step into his embrace.

In a smooth move, he lifted her and set her on the

edge of the table. She gasped in surprise as the stone chilled through the denim of her jeans.

"Okay?" he asked.

"Absolutely." She clutched his shoulders and pulled him to her for a kiss, mouths and tongues meeting in the familiarity of lovers who'd explored each other thoroughly. Well, as thoroughly as they could in such a short time. Breaking off with more than a little regret, she touched her tender lips as if to hold in the sensation of him.

As she leaned away, she heard a rustle beside her and realized he was opening the pastry bag. She eased back to see…Royce tearing off a corner of the pastry and stirring it through a cup of berry jam.

Hmm… Her senses came alive at the scent and at the playful glint in his intense eyes. He was such a delicious contradiction, never ceasing to surprise her. How much more was there to learn about this man?

He brought the bite to her mouth and she opened, but then he popped it into his own mouth playfully. As he chewed though, he pinched off more for her and offered it up. She angled forward for the taste, teasing her tongue along his fingers. Her eyes slid closed at the burst of flavor, sweet fruit and salty him. His pupils widened in response to a last flick of her tongue.

She thrust aside the pastries and tucked her hands into the back pockets of his jeans, digging in her fingers. *Closer*, she willed him. Needed him. Until he stepped between her knees and kissed her again, openmouthed and fully.

Her senses sharpened, the taste of him, the scrape of his unshaven face under her fingers. The crisp scent of Alaskan air on a man filling her every breath. Hmm… And thinking of him filling her sent her mind reeling again.

His hand slid under her sweater, his touch warm and raspy along her flesh. He tunneled farther, sweeping the lamb's wool up and over her head. He growled low in appreciation, cupping her breasts, his approval of red satin quite clear. Her nipples went hard, her skin everywhere tightening with a need for more of this touch, more of him.

Clamping her legs around his waist, she locked him nearer, lost in the connection she'd been aching to recapture. Arching toward him, she pressed for a fuller joining and, yes, thank goodness, yes—he took the hint. His hands slid behind her and freed her bra in a deft sweep.

She made fast work of the buttons in his flannel shirt, sweeping it off his broad shoulders. She flung the body-warmed fabric across the room to rest on top of her sweater. Her fingers trembled, her ache for him so intense. She fumbled with the top button and zipper on his jeans while he tugged her jeans over her hips, lifting her briefly, then pulled the fabric along her legs.

She took the moment to soak in the sight of him.

His washboard stomach gleamed in the sunshine. She reached to trace down, down, down farther still, following the crisp sprinkling of hair in a narrowing trail to his freed button, the V of his open zipper.

Royce flung her pants to the floor and stepped closer. The marble felt cool and slick against the backs of her bare legs. Only her satin panties separated her from total exposure. Her eager hand freed his arousal and his eyes slid closed. He flattened a palm on the counter for a second as if to steady himself.

A surge of feminine power curled through her as she stroked him, her thumb rolling over the first pearly glisten. His throat worked in a long swallow before he opened his eyes. The intensity, the raw passion in his gaze left her breathless.

With slow deliberation, he swiped two fingers through the cup and traced a small swirl of jam over one of her nipples, following to clean the fruit away with his mouth. The warmth of his tasting tongue and the cool air on her wet skin provided the most delicious contrast. He nipped the last taste, sending sparks of pleasure crackling through her. Then he scooped more of the jam, eyeing her lower, lower still, with only a hint of warning that he intended to…

*Yes.*

He eased her back to lie down on the table, her legs dangling. He twisted the edges of her panties in his grip until the satin snapped. Cool air swept over her heated core. Kneeling, he guided her legs over his shoulders. Then… Ahh…

The touch of his finger circled her tight bundle of nerves for tantalizing moments before he replaced the sensation with his mouth. Desire spread throughout her body. Her head fell back as he laved, his undivided attention on her. The gentle sucking along her skin, the light rasp of his tongue, sent shivers of pure pleasure down her spine. She gripped the edge of the marble tabletop, her fingernails sinking in deep.

Her release came hard and fast, rocking through her. She bit her bottom lip to hold back the cry of release as shower after shower of shimmers spread through her.

"You," she gasped simply. "I want you."

Standing, he nipped over her shoulder to draw on her bottom lip. "You are a fantasy come true."

His words sent a thrill along her spine. Her heart tripped over itself in anticipation of more. Of him.

He inched her hips nearer to the edge. "Condoms or no condoms? I'm clean. There's been nobody in a year."

A year? His words, along with the thick pressure of him, right there, so close teased her perilously near completion again.

"Go ahead," he urged, "surrender. I'll take you there as many times as you wish."

His bold confidence sent a charge through her, reminding her of how he'd coaxed her to let go before. And she realized he was in complete control of this moment between them. A thought that called for contemplation when she wanted nothing less than to think.

She banned all other thoughts from her mind but the here and now.

"There is no need for a condom. None. It's only you and me."

Growling, he leaned over her, his hand flat on the table by her ear. Her fingers dug deeper into his flanks as he thrust inside, his low growl of possession echoing through the spacious kitchen. Clamping her legs around his waist again, she urged him deeper, faster. Still she wanted more of him, no holding back. She whispered her wants, even her fantasies, into his ear, delighting in the feel of his throbbing response to her words.

She lost herself in the frenzy of the moment. Nothing could compare to the intensity she felt now in his arms. For a moment, she could forget there was an outside world, concerns for her future in the company, for providing stability for her child.

Royce brought her just shy of release again and again until their bodies slicked with sweat. The musky scent of them together blended with the sweet stickiness of the raspberries and sugary fruit juice.

Locking her ankles tighter behind him, she inched closer and rolled her hips against his. They'd lost the isolation of the retreat, but for this moment at least she had him to herself again. She didn't have to think about all the chaos and fear in her life.

His pulse throbbed in his neck. He dipped his head to her breasts, increasing her pleasure with a flick of his tongue. The tingling in her veins gathered low and pulsed, tighter still until she gasped. Then again.

She couldn't hold back the moan and, thankfully, he quickly kissed her, took her cries of release in his mouth. She bowed upward and into his arms as he thrust again, again, again, until finishing with a hoarse shout muffled against her neck. Her arms went limp with exhaustion around him. She tried to hold on, but her body had melted with weightless bliss. Royce's hold on her tightened and he swept her into his arms.

Sleep pulled at her, pushed her eyelids down. In waves, she faded further and further away from consciousness. The exhaustion from all the stress finally catching up to her, making her bone tired, worries racing to catch up with her again.

Naomi felt Royce carry her to bed for a nap, and the flashes of reality melted into her dreams.

In Alaska, late winter sunsets never ceased to dazzle as if to make up for the fact they came so early half the year. But this? Damn. He'd have a helluva hard time beating this one.

Tessie walked up to the glassed-in balcony, sniffing the air three times before losing interest and setting off in a half prance to explore the rest of the suite.

Royce felt content on the reclining cream sofa at the center of the temperature-controlled sunroom. A dance of vibrant oranges and reds soaked the mountains, casting the landscape in a fiery blaze.

And while the view was damn impressive— breathtaking even—it was the woman in his lap that made his pulse quicken. Instilled that sense of wonder.

Naomi curled up against him, a silk black robe draped over her curves. He adjusted it slightly, careful not to let the strands of her dark hair catch under his arm.

Making love to her again had seriously complicated things between them. But then he suspected nothing with Naomi would ever be simple. Protectiveness hampered things too, given her independence. And if he did act on the impulse to work for her family's company, he would have to figure out what to do about their relationship. Quickly.

He stroked her long hair, letting the silky strands glide between his fingers. "Is your family going to come looking for us?"

"No, we live separate lives here, each of us with our own quarters. We're all adults, who happen to be related. The lodge feels like condos. We all come and go as we please, but the communal areas still make it easier to have business meetings here if need be."

"Sounds like an efficient setup."

"It is." She angled back to look at him. "Were you serious about considering joining the company?"

"I'm considering it," he answered simply.

She nodded, looking away again. "I know our setup here may seem strange to you since you come from a small family. But we're all close, for so many reasons."

He stayed silent, sensing her need to talk. Her family had been through so much, and they were going through hell now.

Naomi toyed with the belt on her robe. "When

all of us were kids, Dad would wake us up early on Saturday mornings. He would caution us to be extra quiet, to tiptoe so we didn't disturb Mom. We'd all bundle up and go to Kit's Kodiak Café." Her tensed muscles relaxed against him with every word. "Best food in the world. We kids would order off the Three Polar Bears Menu. We always ordered the same thing—reindeer sausage, eggs and tall stacks of pancakes served with berry syrup."

He pressed a kiss to her temple. "Your dad sounds like a great guy."

"Yes, he is, very down-to-earth in spite of his wealth. Mom and Dad were emphatic about wanting us to grow up with values, no silver spoon. We had to make our own way in the world."

For a moment, he wondered if she was still working to win him over with stories about her rich but "regular folks" family story. Yet, with all the stress she was under, he couldn't bring himself to confront her on that. "Your father is quite a legend around here. I look forward to meeting him."

"He really is a good man. A little gruff sometimes, but good. After Mom and Brea died, he struggled though. Uncle Conrad stepped in to run the company. Dad became…lost. And so terrified something would happen to us. We had bodyguards, nannies…"

"And then you got sick."

"I was so scared. He'd only just started to come back to us."

"You were scared about him? You were a teen

with cancer. You had every right to be scared for yourself."

"Oh, I was. And the staff was great in helping me deal with that. They helped me keep myself together around the family."

"Naomi… I'm sorry. You should have had your mom, your dad, everyone around you."

"I'm here, and I'm tough." A twist in his arms and suddenly, her face was inches from his, lingering in the space between a kiss. With a wicked grin resting on those plump lips, she kissed him once, twice, nipping and even teasing a hint.

He cupped her head, deepening the kiss.

The kiss held the promise of something more. Or would have. If not for the sound of the elevator bell. And damn, the privacy door had been left open. Two distinctly masculine coughs echoed through the open door between the sunroom and her sitting area.

The separate suites in her family's lodge-style mansion afforded a certain level of privacy, but bottom line, much of her family did still live in the same house. He was so used to a solo life, this blended lifestyle felt alien to him.

Bracing for a confrontation, Royce glanced up fast to find… Hell. Naomi's brothers Marshall and Aiden closing in fast.

Surprise glinted in Marshall's eyes as he tucked his hands into his jeans pockets, his plaid shirt untucked. "Sorry to interrupt, sis. I came to say hello. I didn't realize you were, uh, entertaining."

Naomi gasped, rushing to stand.

And promptly swayed, her knees folding. Royce rushed to brace her but her eyes were already closing as she passed out. She eluded his grasp, collapsing back onto the sofa.

Panic pumping through him, Royce knelt beside her, checking her pulse, stroking her soft face. "Naomi? Naomi, honey…"

Marshall moved to the end of the sofa, swinging her feet up and placing a pillow under them. Teenage Aiden shuffled back and forth in a youthful fidget of indecision.

The million reasons for her fainting entered Royce's head—all of which focused on pregnancy complications. More panic burned in his veins. He looked to Marshall. "Someone call a doctor."

Her older brother sat on the armrest, a hand on his sister's propped feet. "Let's give her a second to wake up before we go all ballistic."

Sighing at the inevitable, Royce knew he would have to betray Naomi's trust. "You don't understand. She's pregnant."

# Ten

Royce wanted to focus all his thoughts on Naomi, but logic was tough to find with his brain on fire with the image of her fainting.

Having all her relatives swarming around him didn't help. Neither had his impulsive revelation about her pregnancy. She would be mad as hell at him, no question. But they needed to know.

Naomi was coming around, sitting up on the sofa, hand resting on her forehead. Royce sat carefully beside her on the cream-colored sofa.

His Saint Bernard was the only mellow one in the room, sprawled out by the wall of windows, soaking up the sun. Naomi's brother—Royce searched for the name of the guy who'd just flown in—Marshall walked forward one thudding step at a time. "What the hell? You knocked up my sister and have the gall to come here, like this, now when our family is going through personal hell?"

Broderick clapped a hand on Royce's shoulder, leveling a laser stare at him. "I think we need to have a…talk."

Aiden hung back watching, quiet, but clearly the teen was ready to throw himself into the fray with one word from his brothers.

Royce stood, keeping an eye on Naomi even as he addressed the trio of brothers. "I realize you're under stress, but you should seriously consider removing that hand. Now."

"How about this?" Broderick's voice rose with every word. "I'll remove any job offer that may have come your way."

Glenna squeezed her husband's elbow. "Broderick, stop. Think of your sister."

Broderick winced, guilt in his eyes. Royce nodded tightly and returned his attention to Naomi. She still looked foggy but she was coming around fast. Fast enough that he could see her fiery temper filling her eyes.

Royce rubbed her shoulder. "Naomi, relax, I've got this."

Naomi shook her head and dark thick hair swished against black silk. "No, *I* have this. I have my life." Her chin tipped as she faced her family. "I'm pregnant because of in vitro fertilization from an anonymous donor. I wasn't ready to tell the family yet since it's still early, just two months along. Royce had nothing to do with this. Our, uh, relationship came as a surprise to both of us. And that's all you get to know."

Broderick extended a conciliatory hand. "Naomi, I'm sor—"

Naomi silenced him with a glare. With a lawyer's precision, she broke their gaze, turned to Glenna, eyes softer now. "Glenna, could you please deal with my Cro-Magnon brother? He's yours now, after all."

"Of course I will." Glenna placed a hand on Broderick's elbow. "But we did come to your suite for a reason. We wanted to let you know that your father's surgery has been set for tomorrow morning."

Royce turned quickly to Naomi just as she all but deflated, her face filling with concern. The scientist in him didn't miss a beat. He put his arm protectively around her shoulders.

No matter what all this family had to say about it—or even how much Naomi might protest—Royce wasn't going anywhere.

For the first time since she woke up from fainting, the jumbled uncase in her stomach wasn't from her pregnancy. Too quickly, fear for her father had come back to the fore.

How could she have forgotten for even a moment?

Unable to resist, she curved into the comfort of Royce's hard-planed body, his steady breaths soothing.

She lost track of how long they sat in silence, Tessie stretched at the base of the sofa. For a moment, Naomi allowed herself to imagine Tessie here long term, running headlong in the pasture below where a bay horse galloped now, kicking up snow and leaving trails of hoofprints.

But then her gaze strayed from the pasture to the water, where the family seaplane bobbed in the waves, tied to the dock. A reminder that her brother Marshall had rushed home. She wasn't ready to think about her father or the mess of everyone hearing about her pregnancy just as they'd discovered her relationship with Royce wasn't all business. She just couldn't go there in her mind. Not yet.

As if sensing the loop of her thoughts, Royce pulled her closer, his arm wrapping around her chest. "I imagine it's tough to think about anything except tomorrow, but let's try." He massaged her shoulders, his jeans warm against her fleece-lined leggings. "I want you to imagine we can go anywhere right now. Where would you want to go? Don't think too hard. Just answer."

Her mind took flight. "Kayaking with whales."

"Seriously?" His laugh rumbled against her lightly. "You wouldn't pick somewhere warm to laze by the beach in the sun?"

"Is Texas boy freezing his toes off in those boots?" she teased.

His laugh—the feel of it tangled up with hers—lingered. "I'm just surprised."

"I love my home state." And she did. So deeply it was a part of her. She glanced back to the Inuit rugs on her floor. Her thoughts went to her heritage, to her mother and all that was already lost.

"Yes, but you're also a glamour girl." He stroked her loose hair.

"Winter clothes are fun too, and more layers to peel away." She tunneled her fingers between the buttons on his shirt, stroking his T-shirt underneath.

"True enough." He slid a palm beneath her loose tunic with deft familiarity that stoked fissions of warmth through her.

"Honestly, I get to travel wherever I want, and I've enjoyed the trips, but I still always look forward to coming home. Maybe part of that is because my family's all here. There's nothing I wouldn't do for them." Her family was woven into her soul, into the fabric of this community and the way she understood the world.

"Clearly. You braved a bear for them."

The bear. A helluva stunt. And one that felt like a distant memory, despite being only a few days ago. Tragedies were funny things like that. Compressing the weariness of years and months into moments. "That seems a lifetime ago."

"A lot has happened in a short time." He drew her closer. "Your father is going to be alright. Just relax and let the doctors do their work. Let me be here for you."

"Releasing control is easier said than done." A sigh tumbled free.

"Control over anything?"

"What about you? You want me to trust you, but

that goes both ways. We've rushed so much and still have so much to learn about each other."

He tensed against her as if it was all he could do to stay on the sofa. But she'd already seen how determined he was to remain by her side. With her father's surgery looming, she doubted Royce would go anywhere.

But afterward?

She shoved aside that thought. "So, do you mind if I ask more about you?"

"What else do you want to know?"

"I'd like to hear more about your former fiancée."

He cricked his neck from side to side, pulling his arm from along the back of the sofa. "She was the girl next door, but also an outsider like me. We both were a few grades ahead in school and, being younger than the rest of the crowd, that made it natural for us to hang out together, eat lunch together, walk home from school together."

"That's quite a history to have…and lose."

His dark eyes went distant, as if he was somewhere else, another place, another time. "When she put the pieces of her life back together again after the miscarriage, she decided to sever all ties to the past. She said she was too dependent on me. Which is damn ironic because I always knew she carried me through life, taught me how to navigate the world, from school onward."

"I'm so sorry." Naomi paused, searching his eyes, unable to resist asking her question, nervous about how important his answer would be to her. "Do you still love her?"

"That's irrelevant. We've been apart for ten years. She's married with three kids."

She couldn't help noticing he'd dodged her question. "Alright, so she's moved on, but that doesn't answer my question. Do you still love her?"

"I can't love anyone who would turn their back on me."

"That's very clear-cut."

"I'm a scientist. I deal better in facts. You should understand that as a lawyer, a person of reason."

"I see so many shades of gray in my job it defies description." A yawn interrupted her. Exhaustion tugged at her after her long night at the hospital and everything that came after.

And she knew Royce wouldn't miss the telltale sign of her tired state. Still she insisted even as her eyes drifted closed, "I want to visit my father again later, when everyone's not vying for his attention."

"I'll wake you."

Surrendering control wasn't easy…but her body won over her will.

For now.

Royce knew that his place was not inside the room with Naomi and Jack Steele, the patriarch of the Alaska Oil Barons dynasty. He knew that. Logic screamed it. Naomi needed time with her father to talk before his surgery.

But damn. He found it hard to stay at the threshold of the hospital door and not be there physically beside Naomi when he knew she needed support.

So he'd settled for the next best thing. Standing at the doorway to eavesdrop.

Not that he coded it that way. Royce preferred to think of it in more scientific terms: *data collection*. Since he couldn't be in there with her, Royce would make sure he knew how to best attend to that beautifully strong-willed force of nature after she left the room.

Jack had a voice like a gale force wind. Even sick and worn, his cadence demanded attention. "I hear from your brother that you're pregnant?"

"Domestication has turned Broderick into a blabbermouth." Though her back was to him, Royce could hear the eye roll in Naomi's assessment of her brother. "But yes, Daddy. I am." She sat in the chair at his bedside. "I'm sorry you didn't hear it from me. I had planned to tell you myself tonight. I wanted you to know before the surgery."

"This guy, the scientist with you? He's the father?" Jack Steele's gaze went to the door where Royce stood reading his cell phone, tamping down a wince over the assumption he was the father.

Broderick hadn't told his dad the details? Apparently, he only spilled part of secrets. Or maybe Jack's concussion was messing with his memory.

"No, Dad, he's not. I went the in vitro route. You're going to be a grandfather. That's good news." Naomi squeezed her dad's hand. "This wasn't how I'd planned for you to find out, but I'm glad you're happy."

"Yes, baby girl. I am. I'm just surprised, and the concussion has me thinking slower than usual. I'm happy for you, for all of us."

"Thank you." Silence echoed heavily before she continued, "I'm sorry I couldn't be the conventional daughter you want."

Naomi's words gutted Royce.

"Whoa, stop with that." Jack lifted a shaky hand to pat his daughter's cheek.

"I didn't mean to upset you. Just rest." She kissed his forehead. "Love you, Daddy."

"Well, just so you know, I like that scientist. Now could you find Jeannie for me?"

Royce could see a hint of resentment sneak past her defenses. But she smiled anyway. "Of course. I'll let her know you're ready for her to come back in."

She stood, tightening her ponytail, then flipping it over her shoulder in an attempt at normalcy. Royce could see her hurt and disappointment in the way her face tightened. The line of her smile and her dark brown eyes said everything, betrayed her disappointment at her father's lukewarm reaction to her news. He couldn't help but think about her apologizing for not being the kind of daughter she thought her father wanted.

And damn if Royce couldn't help but wonder if that had played into why she'd thrown herself in front of a grizzly bear just to meet him.

# Eleven

Wind whipped around the corner of the hospital balcony, covered but not enclosed, stinging Naomi's exposed skin. Wrapping her arms around herself, she tried to push more warmth into her body. The thick cable knit of her green sweater valiantly sheltered her from much of the wind's relentless impact. A day in the thirties in Alaska felt downright balmy.

Normally she embraced the support of her large family, but right now she felt a hint of understanding for Royce's need for solitude. The waiting room had been so packed with people and riotous emotions, everyone worrying about how Jack's surgery was going. Not just family, but friends, as well. People from work. Even a surprise visit from Birch Montoya. He'd quietly kept his distance, while offering support by keeping everyone supplied with coffee.

Naomi's brain and heart were on overload. She'd made sure they knew where to find her and she had her cell phone.

As she inhaled, drinking in the wind, an acute sharpness wedged into her chest. Palpable, locatable fear and unease from a legion of sources.

She needed this moment. This space away from everyone. Part of the allure of Alaska that struck true to Naomi's heart was the iced aloofness of the landscape. Though a delicate ecology existed, there were ways in which the Alaskan brush protected the individual's need for sovereignty and solitude.

Which she needed now more than ever. Waiting for news of her father's surgery had set her on edge, then to feel she fell short of his expectations yet again? That hurt and she didn't know how to reconcile the pain. Heaven help her if something happened to her dad before she found peace with him.

She'd retreated out here since all her siblings had channeled their anxieties over Jack Steele's surgery into a discussion of her pregnancy, with sidelong glances that insinuated she'd gone off on a lark.

No wonder she hadn't told them ahead of time.

The attention felt suffocating. But then her siblings were likely falling into old habits out of stress, focusing on her health and her father's as if their concern could somehow keep death from lashing out prematurely at their family yet again.

From behind her, the rustle of an opening door intruded on her thoughts. Out of the corner of her eye, Royce approached, clothed in a warm jacket, a rough five o'clock shadow taking up residence on his angled face. Her attention remained ahead, extending to the mountain range in front of her that watched over deep sapphire water.

A feeling of conflict rose as a lump in her throat. On one hand, she wanted to melt into Royce's embrace. Cast her fears of intimacy aside and believe he'd be there to support her. He was here listening to her with unjudging eyes when the rest of her family wasn't. But leaning on the railing, she chewed her lip, the fear for her father coalescing with the fear of depending on Royce.

"I just needed some air." She put on her best smile to keep him from whipping out a five-course meal here on the balcony, which was actually kind of sweet. If she could just believe he had faith in her ability to stand on her own. "I assume you of all people understand about the need for some quiet."

"Here's your jacket."

"Thank you. That's thoughtful, but it's actually a fairly warm day for us Alaskans, Texas boy."

"If you're sure." He didn't sound convinced. At all. "Food? Whatever you're craving, I'll find it."

"I'm too upset to eat, but thank you." She couldn't help but notice how he was standing there holding her jacket for her, at her side when no one else in her family was. "I appreciate your effort, but can we just relax?"

"I'm worried about you. Is that so wrong?" He walked toward her, a dusting of snow packing with each step. He stopped beside her, leaning against the railing. Face so near to hers.

Again, Naomi felt torn by the urge to reach out coupled by the urge to run. "You're concerned and that's kind of you. But there's nothing you can do to help my father. Just being here is comfort."

"You've been running yourself ragged with the trip up during the storm and now with your dad's injury." He tucked a windswept strand of her hair behind her ear.

While she recognized he had a point, his observation grated on her nerves, sparking a different kind of fire between them. "I am an adult—" she waved her hand as if gesturing to all of her family members "—with lots of support. And I do mean a lot." Although so far, they hadn't been as supportive as she'd hoped. She wanted to think it was because of distraction over their dad's accident. Time would tell.

"I realize that, but you're tired and stressed. It's icy out here." He had a point, but the way he said it... "What if you were to slip while you're alone?"

"Royce, could you please just—"

The doors swooshed open, cutting her short. Trystan Mikkelson burst through. His rugged, usually reserved face shone with a smile. "We tried texting you."

She patted her sweater pockets and realized... "I, uh, I must have left my phone inside."

How could she have been so careless? She braced herself for the news, almost afraid to accept the hope Trystan's smile brought. Royce moved closer, squeezing her hand in support.

"So I gathered. I am actually the bearer of good news. Your father's surgery went well. He's out. Moving his toes. He will be allowed visitors in about a half hour." Trystan's shaggy hair lifted with a gust of wind that rocked through the balcony.

Naomi's knees went weak, and if she hadn't been leaning against Royce she probably would have slid to the ground. "Thanks, we'll be in shortly."

Trystan nodded, folding back into the hospital, leaving her alone with Royce once again.

Naomi tipped her face into the coolness of the breeze, relief warming her down to her core. "Thank God."

Royce palmed her back. "That's great news."

His touch left her vulnerable at a time when she was clinging to calm by a thread. That's all Naomi had been clutching for days, and that thread rapidly frayed. She couldn't so much as stumble. Not in front of him.

As a child, Naomi rambled when nerves overpowered her. That old habit manifested again as she desperately tried to gain a firmer grip on her emotions. "Dad's recovery will take about six weeks, then rehab, but it's so much better than the old days of needing that metal halo for six months."

"Let's go to the cafeteria and get something to eat while you wait to see him."

She bit back the urge to snap at him, frustration firing deep inside her now that the pressure from her father's surgery was gone. She was tired and cranky and, yes, still irritated with him for telling her family about her pregnancy.

What right did he have to do that? To take that moment away from her? Somehow, she'd lost sight of the impact of that when she'd been groggy from fainting. Afraid for her child. Terrified for her father.

She couldn't let that pass. He couldn't take over her life this way.

This wasn't the time or the place to tell him, with her emotions still too raw for logic, her feelings bubbling to the surface. "Royce, I'm not hungry." She stuffed her hands into the sleeves of her sweater, refusing to admit that, yes, she was getting cold. "I don't mean to snap, but I'm an adult. I'm not going to fall off the balcony, and I can feed myself. Drive myself. Keep myself upright."

Royce drew in a deep breath, his jaw tight before he spoke, "And you have a reckless streak."

Her eyebrows shot upward.

"Excuse me?" So much for resisting snapping. Logic, reason, calmness—all lost somewhere on that breeze. He'd laid down fighting words. Same ones she'd pushed against her whole life.

"You're impulsive."

"Perhaps it just feels that way since you're so methodical— Forget I said anything. I'm going back inside." She wheeled away from him.

And her feet shot out from under her.

Royce caught her just shy of her hitting the ground. "See, you do need me. Think about your baby."

Anger fired hot inside her. She loved her baby. How dare he insinuate otherwise? "That's not fair. Do you plan to stay plastered to my side for the next seven months?"

"Calm down. You're being irrational."

She leveled her best courtroom gaze his way— and yes, she had inherited more than her fair share of her father's bravado. "Oh, so I'm impulsive and irrational?"

"You're playing lawyer, twisting my words."

"If you ask me, you're the one whose emotions are out of control. You blurted to my family that I'm pregnant. You stole that once-in-a-lifetime chance for me to tell them about my first child."

"I was worried for you." He shot back.

"I'm not your fiancée." The woman he'd loved. A thought that burned through her, bringing an ugly green jealousy to the fore. "This isn't the past."

His head jerked back. "That's a low blow."

"I can't help how I feel, or how it seems that you're using our relationship to reconcile what happened before."

"And I think you're overreacting because of how your family treated you when you had cancer. Maybe you're even pushing me away because of the people you've lost, or some fear of trusting the future. Hell, I don't know for sure. I'm not the word expert like you are."

"Wow, well, you're certainly off to a great start."

She crossed her arms tightly. "It's clear we've made a mistake. The storm is over."

"You're pushing me away. Point proved."

"If that's the way you want to see it." She braced a hand along a rail and backed away from him. "I'm going to see my father. I can find my own ride home."

Angling past him, she made her way inside. Just in time to see her father being wheeled past on a gurney by a middle-aged nurse. He groggily sang lyrics to old '50s songs, his tone loopy. On another day, Naomi's heart might have burst with laughter at the goofy display.

Instead, tears burned in her eyes and an ache filled her heart. She wanted to cry her eyes out over the realization that the fear she'd felt when she'd *wanted* to lean on Royce, the stab of jealousy she'd felt, was for a reason… She'd fallen for the man she'd just shoved out of her life for good.

Delaney raced down the hospital corridor to catch Birch before he made it to the elevator. Keeping her eyes on his broad shoulders in the crowded hallway, she angled past a nurse pushing a vitals monitor down the hall. She could still hardly believe he'd shown up here.

At first, she'd been afraid he would push the issue of sharing the truth about their relationship when she was feeling too scared and vulnerable to resist. But he'd kept his distance, hadn't given so much as a hint of their affair, simply stating he'd come because he respected Jack.

Birch had been such a steady source of support as she waited to hear about her father's surgery. Although every now and again, she could have sworn his eyes had broadcast his frustration at keeping his distance. Others wouldn't have seen it. But she knew him too well now.

Once the doctor had told them Jack was out of surgery, in recovery but not awake, Birch had said his farewells. Relief had taken the wind right out of Delaney so intensely, she'd almost missed the chance to catch him. And that made her feel guilty as hell after the way he'd come to check on her.

At the elevator, she rested a hand lightly on his arm as he pushed the button. She kept her touch neutral, too aware that someone could see them, but needing to thank him for being so thoughtful. He was a good man in many ways. "That was nice of you to stop by the hospital to check on my father."

"It's what people who care about each other do," he said tightly, pointedly.

She shifted, guilt pinching. Looking around at the people gathered at the elevator, she tugged Birch's elbow, leading him with her to a tucked away corner with two chairs. Thank goodness he didn't resist, only gestured for her to sit first and then took his place beside her.

"You have something to tell me?" he asked simply.

"I know you wanted something more from me back there, but it just didn't seem like the right time to…"

"To what? To let people know we've been together for over two months? Although I'm not sure what to call whatever we have going on. What are we exactly?"

Tension pulled tighter inside her, shoulders bracing.

"My father just went through a life-threatening surgery. Cut me a little slack."

"That's why I am here. To support you. You can't intend to keep us a secret forever."

"Of course not."

"Good. Let me be here for you. I can get coffee, we can sit with your sister and Royce."

The possibility of such a gathering sounded… happy. Good. She bit her lip against the hope.

Birch continued, "Maybe Miller might have worked a miracle with some kind of modifications for the pipeline that won't bankrupt the company."

She knew he meant it as an attempt to ease the tension with a joke, and maybe her emotions were too sensitive at the moment, but just that fast, Birch dashed her hopes of his ability to see her side of things. "Sure."

"You mean that?" The skepticism in his tone told her he'd heard the undercurrent in her voice. The pulling away.

"When the time is right." She'd been using the same delay tactic for weeks, knowing it wouldn't last forever.

"We've been sleeping together for over two

months." His dark eyes flashed with a new fire. "We've known each other for a helluva lot longer." He took her hand in his. "When's the right time?"

She swallowed past the fear, wishing she could fall into the promise in his gaze. Knowing that would be beyond foolish. Licking her lips, she peered around to make sure no one they knew was nearby while they held hands this way. "Be honest. Where do you see this relationship going with how very different we are?"

He let go of her, his jaw flexing. "I thought I made myself clear. I want us to go public, to meet each other's friends and families." He paused. "But I can see in your face that's not something that interests you."

Panic made her stomach ache. She hadn't wanted things to end like this, but she couldn't lie to him about a future together, either. "I just can't envision how we'll blend our worlds."

"You're dumping me because I would embarrass you in front of your friends?"

She flinched at the word *dumping*. She'd known this couldn't last forever, but thinking about ending their affair was tougher than she'd expected. "I'm saying I can't imagine how we'll blend our very different beliefs."

"Let me get this straight. If I don't agree with you on everything, we can't be together. Look at your sister and Miller."

"It's not that simple. Not for me, at least."

"Then explain it to me."

"Of course, people in a relationship can disagree about a lot of things. But there are some core values we can't compromise on." She searched his eyes and could see he still didn't understand. "What if I asked you to give up your holdings in companies that are harming the environment?"

She held her breath, knowing he'd refuse. But then again...what if he didn't?

"I wouldn't ask you to give up your job." His dismissiveness chafed.

Still, she gave it another chance, reframing her position.

"I'm not asking you to give up your profession. Just a portion of your holdings."

"It's not that simple—"

She couldn't help but notice how his words echoed hers from earlier.

"—people count on me with their futures," he continued. "If I do what you suggest, unrest could ripple through the investors, causing my whole corporation to collapse in a stock market sellout."

His position was expected. But the disappointment that came with it burned so much deeper than she ever could have imagined just a few weeks ago.

"I suspect you're smart enough to figure out a way around that. If you wanted to. But I can see that you don't."

She couldn't compromise on something so intrinsic to her values. Images of her sister's teenage body rav-

aged from cancer treatment haunted her to this day.
Her family had taken one hit after another. She couldn't
give Birch a way to hurt the Steeles too. Not when
she had it in her power to keep him and his business
practices at arm's length. And she couldn't string him
along, either. She cared too much to do that to him.

The time had come to walk away from Birch.

Even if it cost her a broken heart.


Somehow on her way to check on her father,
Naomi had found her steps slowing as she spotted
Jeannie. An urge to stop, talk, comfort the woman
had flooded through her. Crazy. Probably. Jeannie
Mikkelson had four children of her own ready and
eager to hold their mother's hand.

But Naomi had felt drawn to something in the
woman's eyes. Something that sure seemed to echo a
feeling taking root in Naomi's heart for Royce Miller.

To hide the renewed sting of tears, Naomi pulled
her hair clamp free and re-secured her ponytail. The
past two hours since Jack's surgery had been emotional, to say the least. Each member of the Steele
family had filtered in and out, followed by the Mikkelsons, all eager to see him post-op, a sea of concern and relief washing through the room.

Naomi had decided to wait until the end by Jeannie's side since Glenna had left to make sure the
house was ready for everyone to crash. Everyone was
exhausted. Even Delaney had disappeared. And yes,
maybe Naomi was afraid to go home to her solitary

suite, where she feared she would fall apart amid the memory of her time there with Royce.

Jeannie touched her arm, calling Naomi back to the present. Leaning forward, the older woman's blond hair fell on her pink sweater, making her seem younger somehow. Much more together than Naomi felt. "Thank you for hanging out with me, you've been so kind. I'm really okay." She paused, then looked at Naomi with a narrowed gaze. "But are *you* okay?"

Ha. Loaded question for sure. "I'm fine. Just a little tired. This is a day to celebrate."

"Yes, we've had a miracle here with your father's surgery and the wonderful news about your baby. I know that no one will ever replace your mother, but I hope you know I am here to listen if you need me. Family is there for each other."

*Family?* Naomi sat stunned as the word shifted around in her mind and realized, accepted, yes, this merger—a blended family—was going to happen. And before she knew it, words tumbled out of her mouth. "How did you juggle it all? Kids, work, a happy marriage?"

Jeannie laughed, rolling her eyes. "Who said I juggled it?"

"I've heard about you for years, seen the features in magazines." Read them as a teen, poring over the perfect family photos, wondering what it would have been like if her mother had lived. "You had it all, career and family."

"Charles and I loved each other, but make no mistake, we argued," Jeannie said. "All couples do. I made mistakes at work. Heaven knows there are so many things I wish I could go back and redo as a mother, times I wish I'd slowed down to cherish."

"But you still did it all. No one's perfect."

"Exactly, honey. No one's perfect. Quit expecting perfection from yourself—and from Royce."

Naomi leaned forward in the chair. "It's scary to think about, um, failing."

That last word tripped her up, hung in her mind, resonating at the core of so much. Fear of imperfection. Fearing she'd failed her family. That she would cause them more grief. She'd known that cancer wasn't anyone's fault, but to see her father broken all over again so soon after losing his wife and a child?

Naomi's teenage mind had felt the guilt. Clearly some of that had leaked into her adulthood, pushing her to overcompensate.

Jeannie leaned back in her chair, nodding. Considering. Heartbeats of silence passed before she spoke again. "Not trying is scarier."

"Perhaps we're more alike than I realized." Damn straight, Naomi was scared of failing. But Royce? He was worth facing her fear. She realized now that she wanted to fight for him with every ounce of her soul. If only she had some sort of courtroom-style strategy to win him back.

But as experienced as she was in that arena, when it came to love, she could only follow her instincts.

# Twelve

Royce had spent the better part of an hour behind the wheel of the SUV, trying to clear his mind after the fight with Naomi yesterday.

Like Texas, Alaska offered pristine roads, perfect for driving and thinking.

He didn't know how to approach this problem. There was no scientific method to apply. All the variables and moving parts made the situation with Naomi feel impenetrable and unapproachable.

For a man who prided himself on his critical thinking skills, he'd come up empty-handed.

Which was how he ended up back at the Steele compound. Sure, he needed to collect Tessie. But really, he had to admit, he didn't want to leave Naomi like this.

Emerging from the car, he started toward the looming main house, feeling dwarfed beneath the towering architecture. Perhaps it had to do with nerves.

Helluva mess here. His fidgeted with his abacus key chain in his parka pocket.

Trystan Mikkelson intercepted him on the way to the house, nodding. Jeannie's younger son, the rancher, sported cowboy boots and a tall black Stetson, a jacket—wind resistant—designed for riding in this weather. He motioned for Royce to follow him. "Let's nab a couple of Steele horses."

"Sounds good to me."

They walked in silence to the twenty-stall barn, a large red building trimmed by slate stones. Trystan was known as a rugged guy, his lack of polish earning him a behind-the-scenes role in the family.

Making their way to the barn, Royce passed a few of the Steeles and Mikkelsons on horseback, heading out toward the mountain trails. Marshall led the small group. Naomi, he couldn't help but notice, was not a part of the group. Heaven help him if he or anyone suggested she might not want to gallop around while pregnant.

Trystan's somber features seemed more pronounced in this setting, his Stetson shadowing his face. "You do ride, right?"

"I'm from Texas." To his mind, the math was obvious. "I live in Alaska. I ride."

"Let's saddle up, then."

"Wouldn't you rather drive? I would think after Jack's accident you might not be too eager for a horseback ride." Royce looked to the line of stalls. A variety of horses poked their heads out, a seeming perpetual murmur of nickers echoing in the modern barn facility. He wondered which horse was Naomi's. He looked the length and saw sleds, skis and even a horse-drawn sleigh parked in back.

"It wasn't the horse's fault. It was an accident. That could have happened in the car or fishing or walking. Things happen. We can't let accidents keep us from living our lives." Trystan led a sorrel quarter horse with a blaze out of the stall. Handing the animal's leather lead rope to Royce, he gave the horse a pat on the neck. "I've met Phantom before. Shouldn't throw you on your ass."

"Thanks for the vote of confidence." Royce let the sorrel sniff his hand, the whiskers of the gelding tickling his palm. Leading the horse to the cross ties, he looked over at Trystan, who pulled a dapple gray from another stall and led him to another set of cross ties.

Trystan pulled out two currycombs and a hard brush for them to use. Royce grabbed the currycomb, rubbing sinewy shoulders and flanks in circular patterns, loosing dirt and warming up Phantom's muscles.

"Once things settle down with Jack's recovery, I would like to schedule a meeting to speak with both families together. Just to talk." Royce brushed the loosed dirt off Phantom and used a hoof pick to clean out his hooves.

"Naomi was persuasive, huh? She's always been a top-notch negotiator." He took them into the climate-controlled tack room and hoisted an intricate Western saddle, saddle pad and bridle for Royce to grab.

"Actually, it was seeing the Steeles and the Mikkelsons pull together. That integrity made me want to know more about your operation." He'd been considering the move since they'd arrived here, but now… How awkward might it be to work in the company if he and Naomi weren't a couple?

As they exited the tack room, Royce placed a hand on Phantom's haunches, letting the horse know he was there. In a quick motion, he placed the saddle pad and saddle on the gelding and cinched the girth. Keeping one hand on Phantom's neck, he moved up to unhinge the halter from the cross ties. Eschewing the halter, he slipped the sorrel's head into the bridle.

"Let's ride and talk." The dapple gray let out a low nicker as Trystan led him past Phantom and Royce, moving from the barn to the open field.

"Is this a business test of some sort? And if so, shouldn't we be in a boardroom?" Royce followed, clicking his tongue to command his horse to follow. The quarter horse responded with a spirited toss of the head and a prance forward.

They made their way into the open space. Trystan, already seated in the saddle, looked at ease. He leaned on the horn, tipping his Stetson. "I'm not the boardroom sort. Let's call this more of a challenge."

Staying silent, Royce pulled himself up into the saddle adjusting his weight.

"A rite of passage, really—" Trystan urged the dapple forward "—if you expect to be a part of this motley crew."

"I think you have that backward. I'm the one deciding if I want to share my research with your company or another." Squeezing his calves, he prompted Phantom into a working trot.

"I'm not talking about business. I'm talking about the way everyone's blending all these families together. I may not be as diplomatic as the rest of them, but since Naomi's not my sister, I'm also less likely to punch you in the face. So I got nominated to take measure of you. And, well, I guess you'll do." With that, Trystan and the dapple surged forward, kicking off into a headlong gallop. A challenge indeed.

At Royce's whoop, Phantom lunged into a gallop, gaining ground on Trystan. Each stretch of the stride seemed to melt some of the tension away. It'd been too long since his last ride.

After a quarter mile along the beaten path through sprawling trees, Trystan slowed his horse into a loping canter and then a slow trot. Reluctant to disengage from the speed, but eager to see what Trystan meant by his comment, he slowed Phantom down.

"Hmm?" The nonanswer hung in the horse-length distance between them. The sounds of the others riding carried on the wind. The roar of a snowmobile hummed as Aiden drove just ahead.

"What?" Trystan asked. "Nothing to say?"

"I didn't hear a question." A technicality on Royce's part.

Trystan cast a glance backward at the family they'd left behind, then shifted forward in the creaking saddle again. "Are you and my future stepsister seeing each other?"

Such a loaded inquiry. One that made Royce reel. The fight from earlier flashed before his eyes, the fear of losing the woman in his life again, a woman pregnant with a child he was already learning to care about. "No, we're not."

"Man of few words. I like that. But it's obvious to all of us that the two of you have some kind of connection."

"You're a little old for the overprotective stepbrother routine," Royce said drily, stroking Phantom's neck as they slowed to a walk.

Barking out a laugh, Trystan shot him a look. "Clearly you don't have siblings."

"Touché."

"Well, if you are seeing each other—or plan to be seeing each other again—be careful with her. I've been around horses enough to get a sense of things. Naomi's more softhearted under that tough exterior than people think."

"I noticed."

"And there's the baby to consider—as you told everyone."

Royce scratched along his neck, remembering Naomi's pain over how he'd shared her secret before she was ready. "I'm an intelligent man. This is all obvious."

Or rather it should have been.

"Okay, then there's this. Be very certain before you start a relationship with her. My brother Chuck, my future stepbrothers and I outnumber you five to one. Not to mention my baby sister is quiet, but can hold her own in ass-kicking."

Unlike earlier, Royce realized he wasn't looking at data or science at all. He was hearing the words, the way he'd learned from Naomi. He tuned into the nuance. To the way data was framed. The word *outnumbered* echoed in his mind. Outnumbered positioned him as a threat, sure, but also signified to his mind that even as a fully capable and dynamic adult woman, her brothers thought of her in the framework of the teen who was sick with cancer.

Well-intentioned, just as he'd been earlier by insisting she eat, insisting she rest. No wonder her reaction had been so severe. So sharp. She constantly worked to not feel smothered. To not be pampered. She wanted to be taken seriously and seen as strong.

He knew she was strong.

So what could he do to win her back? To prove he could be the man a strong woman like her needed and wanted in her life?

This time, it couldn't be about the numbers or logic. He was going to have to dig deep for what came tougher for him, the part that—because of Naomi—he was learning was crucial.

Because Naomi was his future and if he wanted to win her—and God, he did—then he knew.

He would have to lead with his heart.

Pacing around her loft, Naomi couldn't seem to work out the problem that had nagged at her mind for the past few hours. Guilt over how things went with Royce, how she'd snapped at him, tore at her soul. And yes, it had something to do with the fact that scared her down to the core of her being.

She loved him.

There. That certainty swelled in her chest. It ought to give her relief. But there was still the issue of her needing to be an equal partner, cared for, sure, but not smothered. How could she make things right while ensuring he understood?

*Could* he understand?

Of course, all of that was contingent on him even wanting to see her again after their fight.

Another turn about the room didn't bring on the inspiration of a plan. Nope. She came up empty again. Every apology sounding horrible as she imagined the conversation in her head.

Those thoughts would have to wait. Her cell, which she'd clutched as she paced the room, screamed to life in her hand. Glancing down at the screen, her heart beat out of time.

*Royce.*

For a moment, she'd forgotten he'd placed his number into her phone. And it wasn't just a phone call. He wanted to video chat.

So much for having her plan smoothed out.

She stroked back her hair, breathed in and out to steady herself, then tapped the screen. His dark eyes smoldered, struck into her.

Naomi wished she'd taken in a couple more of those bracing breaths. "Hello. Did you leave something here?"

He gave her a lopsided smile. "As a matter of fact, I did."

Her heart sunk. She'd been hoping… "What is it? Let me know where to look and I'll leave it with one of the staff."

"It's not something you can return, actually."

She searched his face, hoping, and yet still wary of voicing as much. "I'm not sure I understand."

His smile—full-on shining now—made her heart skip a beat.

"Look out of your window, Naomi."

Her window? She walked to the enclosed balcony and…her heavy heart leaped right into her throat.

Royce stood in the snowy yard, with Tessic by his side. Just like something out of a movie. He'd come to her, tall and handsome against the background of glistening trees. She looked at the phone image of him again and wondered why she hadn't recognized the surroundings before. She could hardly believe he was here, after the way she'd pushed him away at the hospital.

Tessie barked once, twice, pulling Naomi's attention back to the phone, back to Royce and the hope that they could rediscover what they'd found at the retreat. "Are you going to stay out there or are you planning to come inside?"

"I could, but actually I had something else in mind. Do you think you could come down so we can talk more about what I left at your place? I would come up there, but I'm fairly sure we'll end up in bed together and there are some things we should discuss."

He was reaching out and from the roguish grin on his face, what he wanted to say was most definitely something she wanted to hear. "I'm on my way down."

She practically tripped over her own two feet as she tugged on her pink parka, snow boots and sheepskin gloves. A blur took her from loft to elevator, barely registering the rest of the compound as determined footfalls led her outside to the chilled air. To Royce.

Flipping up her hood, she raced to where he stood. An enchanted prince against a snowy backdrop. Tessie bounded in the fresh powder to Naomi, tail wagging with anticipation and excitement. Naomi tilted her head, gesturing to the landscape. "Where have you been?"

"Here, actually. I came to get Tessie and ended up going riding with Trystan. It gave me some time to think, get perspective." He extended a hand to her. "Would you like to go on a sleigh ride so we can talk?"

Joy shimmered inside her at his magical offer, all the more special as it was unexpected from the reclusive scientist who claimed his life was all about work.

"You know how to handle a horse and sleigh?" A rhetorical question, really. She was more taken by the fact he'd arranged this for her, for them.

"I've driven a wagon in Texas." He shrugged a shoulder, confidence glinting in his eyes as he stepped closer. "I'm hoping it's the same. But if it's not, I trust my Alaskan companion can teach me how."

Was he serious? He'd been worried about her falling off a balcony, for crying out loud. Would he give her that kind of control?

"You're willing to let me drive?" She said it slowly, wanting to be sure he understood the underlying issue.

She needed to feel like he trusted her to be strong. Capable.

"Of course. I'm trying to send a message here, but in case you haven't noticed, I'm not always as good at emotions as I am at science." He extended his hand again. "But I am trying," he repeated.

This time, she took his hand, and together they made their way toward the barn, snow crunching beneath their feet.

Off to the left was her father's old-fashioned sleigh with two draft horses—Mars and Jupiter—already hitched. Mars shook his head, the rustle of bells filling the air with a hint of holiday cheer in an Alaskan spring.

Climbing into the sleigh, she grabbed the plaid blanket he'd placed on the seat, then waited while he unhooked the horses from the post. Anticipation mounted in her chest. That determined heart of hers no longer feeling heavy, but alive, pounding with excitement.

Stepping into the sleigh, Tessie close at his heels, he passed the leather reigns to her, an earnest gesture.

His gloved hand touched hers in the exchange, that electricity once again growing between them, warming her from the inside. She clicked her tongue, urged the two draft horses forward. The sleigh gained momentum, gliding in the yet untouched snow.

Royce sat next to her under the blanket, his leg touching hers, maintaining contact that almost threatened to distract her from driving and the scenery of a slowly sinking sun behind fresh white land.

Her land. Silence stretched as she enjoyed the view, this pristine beauty that stole her breath as fast as the man beside her. Chunks of ice breaking loose in the water caused the family seaplane to bob, seeming to nod approval at their journey. She could see tracks where her brothers had ridden earlier today. As she passed the tree house she and her siblings had used as children, her heart nearly burst. So many memories here, in this place.

"Naomi." Royce's low voice rumbled like a river through her thoughts, drawing her into the present. The beautiful present. "How's your father doing?"

"Sleeping well, as of when I spoke to Delaney an hour ago. The last nurse's check showed all great vitals. No recurrence of the high blood pressure." She couldn't ask for more. Family was everything, a blessing she hoped to expand with the baby she carried.

And with Royce?

The possibility warmed her far more than any blanket.

"That's good, really good."

Her grip tightened on the reins. "I'm sorry for the way I spoke to you at the hospital."

"You have nothing to apologize for. While I was out with Trystan, I realized something."

"What's that?" She pulled on the left rein with a tug-tug, signaling a change of direction to the horse team, striking out for the trail leading through a bower of snow-laden trees. Her favorite path.

"We moved so fast that while we got the basics, we don't know each other enough to instinctively understand where the other person is coming from," Royce said, resting a gloved hand on her knee.

His touch and words pulled her gaze back to him and she realized no way could she keep her attention on driving any longer. She slowed the horses until they came to a stop with a snort. Tessie, who had been on Royce's other side, hopped out to tunnel through piles of snow in that way of hers that was becoming familiar and dear.

Naomi shifted in her seat to face Royce. "Okay, I can see that. Is that your way of saying you understand I was on edge at the hospital?"

"More than that." He took her hand and linked their fingers, squeezing lightly. "You told me your family smothered you, and I didn't listen, not really."

"You were being thoughtful. I realize that now. And you have your own fears from your past."

"You know those facts, just like I know the facts of what you went through. But fully trusting each other? That takes time." His voice, so strong, filled the cold air with warm puffs.

"Are you saying you want us to take that time?" She needed to hear him say it outright, to be sure she hadn't misunderstood. And yes, maybe she wanted to savor the words, as well.

"Yes, that's what I'm saying." Simple words, but honest and up-front—as this man had always been with her.

She had to clear up one last, but vital, question. "Even though I'm pregnant?"

"Yes. In fact, I seem to recall that I told everyone, when that should have been your news to share.

I apologize for taking that joy from you. I have the reputation as a recluse for a reason. Relationships and communication? Not my strong suit."

"You're doing really well right now. And to be fair, I started things off on the wrong foot between us, not being honest." Guilt pinched her even more than before, now that she knew him, respected him. Loved him. "I should have been honest with you. Now you've been more than fair in how you've dealt with my family. In how you've forgiven me."

"You've had solid reasons for your actions. I understand logic."

She laughed lightly, relieved and glad she'd trekked up the mountain to meet this man on that snowy day. "Thank you. You've made me so very happy."

"It's that simple to make you happy?" he asked, his brilliant eyes a hint bewildered.

"It's a good start." She took his hands. "But what makes you happy?"

"Loving you."

She blinked, swiped snowflakes from her vision and wondered if perhaps she'd heard wrong. No one other than family had ever said that to her. And certainly no one in the romantic sense. She'd given up thinking she'd have this kind of love. She would have never imagined this kind of happiness when she went to that clinic alone to start trying for a baby.

She swallowed down a lump of emotion and asked, needing to hear it again, "What did you say?"

"I said that I love you, Naomi Steele. You blind-sided me from the moment I first saw you in a snow-storm shouting down a bear." His smile dazzled her. "I'm still working on the details of how we fit as a couple, but damn it, I know we have something amazing here. Once-in-a-lifetime amazing, and I want us to work together to build a future together, with the baby— Am I going too fast for you again?"

"Not too fast at all. Just perfect. Absolutely per-fect." She stroked his strong jaw. "I'd been making lists of possible names, but I'm wondering. Would you like to do that together?"

He kissed her hands clasped in his. "I would like that." A wealth of emotion shifted through his deep coffee-brown eyes. He tucked her close, a perfect fit. "What are you thinking?"

As he held her against his side, his arm around her shoulders, she felt at peace for the first time in longer than she could remember. Like she no longer had to run or throw up guards. No. Right here in his strong arms, she felt…at home.

"Actually," she said, blinking back happy tears, "I was just thinking how I wish I had a beautiful speech to offer you in return. I'm the wordsmith, the litiga-tor, after all. But the only words that come to mind are how much I love you too."

Sketching a kiss along her temple, he whispered in her ear, "Sounds like the perfect formula to me."

# Epilogue

*Two weeks later*

Naomi Steele wasn't naive. Her life had brought enough challenges to make her wise—and thanks to knowing and loving Royce Miller, she was no longer jaded.

Curled up beside him on the sofa at the glass igloo where they'd met, she typed on her computer, complete with reliable internet thanks to the permanent satellite Royce had installed when he bought the place. Apparently, those patents of his opened up a lot of choices when it came to where they lived. They'd found this the perfect nostalgic retreat for when the Steele compound noise proved too much for

Royce. Sunshine streamed through the roof, casting prisms along Tessie's fur as the dog slept at Royce's feet.

Naomi and Royce were finding their way through building a relationship and a future. His consulting work for Alaska Oil Barons was invaluable. His strong-willed independence made for a good balance with her family's big personalities.

He'd even accompanied her to her doctor's appointment yesterday and wanted to attend the ultrasound appointment in two weeks. His enthusiasm about the pregnancy was genuine and made her love for him grow.

Royce stroked a lock of her hair, before sliding a hard-muscled arm around her shoulders. "How are you feeling?"

"Like I'm gaining weight at the speed of light." She looked up from her laptop to smile at him. "But so happy."

"It's good to see your father walking around."

Her dad was a bit of an impatient patient, but he was devoting his full effort to rehab. Jeannie had proved to be a godsend in gently but firmly teasing him out of his frustration. Delaney had also stepped up, taking time off work to devote her full attention to their father. There was a hint of sadness in her eyes. But then, the scare with Jack's health had been hard on all of them.

Naomi stroked Royce's bristly cheek. "Have I told

you how much it meant to me having you at my side lately?"

"Being with you is clearly no hardship." He tipped her chin and kissed her, his touch, his mouth, launching tingles to the roots of her hair. Easing back, he tapped the edge of her keyboard. "What are you working on?"

She pulled her thoughts off taking that kiss further—for now—and clicked her computer screen back to life. "Broderick forwarded me an invitation our company received to be featured at a wildlife preservation fund-raiser this summer."

"Whoa." Royce whistled softly. "That's quite a coup. It'll be super press as the merger moves forward. There will be a lot of movers and shakers there, a lot of investors like Birch Montoya."

"Which could bring more capital for your initiatives." She tapped the abacus key chain in his hand. "They just want a commitment from us on a face for the company since Dad's recovering and Jeannie's not leaving his side."

"There are plenty of Steeles and Mikkelsons to choose from." He set aside the key chain on the coffee table. "Although Aiden's clearly too young. And I can't imagine Trystan Mikkelson would want any part of it."

"Thank heavens." She shook her head, then tucked her loose hair behind her ear. "He's great at what he does, managing their family's ranch outside of Juneau, but he's more than a little rough around the edges. He would need an intense makeover to pull off that kind of public role for the company."

"We all have our niche in getting the job done."

"That we do." She looked into his bourbon-brown eyes, the intensity of the man setting her senses on fire.

Her cell phone rang, expanding the world around her. She angled over to read the screen. Her doctor's name scrolled across it.

A hint of concern skittered up her spine. She answered, turning on the speakerphone, then clasping Royce's hand. He squeezed firmly.

"Hello," she answered.

"Miss Steele? This is Dr. Odell's office. I'm his nurse."

"Yes…" She paused, thinking back to her appointment. "Is there a problem with my blood work?"

"Not a problem at all," the nurse continued, a smile in her voice. "We would like to bring you back in for an ultrasound. Your blood serum tests lead us to believe that you're carrying twins."

"Twins?" Royce echoed.

Stunned, Naomi couldn't even speak. Swallowing hard, she looked up at Royce—and found him grinning. The shock eased, joy and wonder sliding in after.

Her hand slid to her stomach and she finally whispered, "Twins."

She shouldn't have been surprised. With twins in her family and having used in vitro, it was a possibility. But she'd been so afraid it wouldn't take at all, this double blessing. Her heart swelled.

The rest of the phone call passed in a blur as the doctor's nurse gave her an appointment time. Which Royce noted in his tablet, thank goodness.

Once the line disconnected, he set aside the device and moved her laptop. "This calls for a celebration."

Excitement over the news mixed with a thrill at his touch skimming down her arm. "What exactly do you have in mind?"

His fingers trailed from her hand to her thigh. "Ice cream."

Her breath hitched in her throat as he stroked up her side, grazing the curve of her sensitive breast. "Ice cream?"

"Together. In bed. Naked. Double scoops for the double deal celebration."

"Hmm," she sighed, arching into his caress. "Lead the way."

He lifted her into his arms and turned toward the bed. "My pleasure."

\* \* \* \* \*

*Notorious playboy Nolan Madaris is determined
to escape his great-grandmother's famous
matchmaking schemes, but Ivy Chapman, the
woman his great-grandmother has picked out
for him, is nothing like he expects—and she's got
her own proposal for how to get their meddling
families off their backs and out of their love lives!*

*Read on for a sneak peek of
BEST LAID PLANS,
the latest in* New York Times *bestselling author
Brenda Jackson's*
MADARIS FAMILY SAGA!

# Prologue

*Christmas Day*

Nolan Madaris III took a sip of his beer while standing on the balcony of his condo. Leaning against the rail, he had a breathtaking view of the exclusive fifteen-story Madaris Building that was surrounded by a cluster of upscale shops, restaurants and a beautiful jogging park with a huge man-made pond. The condos where he lived were right across from the water.

The entire complex, including the condos, had been architecturally designed, engineered and constructed by the Madaris Construction Company that was owned by his cousins Blade and Slade. For the holidays, the Madaris Building and the surrounding shops, restaurants and jogging park were beautifully decorated with colorful, bright lights. It was hard to believe a new year was just a week away.

When Nolan had arrived home from his cousin Lee's wedding, he hadn't bothered to remove his tuxedo. Instead he'd headed straight for the refrigerator, grabbed a beer and proceeded to the balcony for a bit of mental relaxation. But all his mind could do was recall the moment his ninetysomething-year-old great-grandmother, Felicia Laverne Madaris, had finally cornered him at the reception that evening. She was a notorious matchmaker, and he'd been avoiding her all night. Her success rate was too astounding to suit him—and she had calmly warned him that he was next.

He was just as determined not to be.

Nolan, his brother, Corbin, and his cousins Reese and Lee had all been born within a fifteen-month period. They were as close as brothers and had been thick as thieves while growing up. Mama Laverne swore her goal was to marry them all off before she took her last breath. They all told her that wouldn't happen, but then the next thing they knew, Reese had married Kenna and today Lee married Carly.

What bothered Nolan more than anything about his great-grandmother setting her schemes on him was that she of all people knew what he'd gone through with Andrea Dunmire. Specifically, the hurt, pain and humiliation she had caused him. Yes, it had been years ago and he had gotten over it, but there were some things you didn't forget. A woman ripping your heart out of your chest was one of them.

His cell phone rang. Recognizing the ringtone, he pulled it out of his pocket and answered, "Yes, Corbin?"

"Hey, man, I just wanted to check on you. We saw you tear out of here like the devil himself was after you. It's Christmas and we thought you would stay the night at Whispering Pines and continue to party like the rest of us."

Whispering Pines was their uncle Jake's ranch. Nolan took another sip of his beer before saying, "I couldn't stay knowing Mama Laverne is already plotting my downfall. You wouldn't believe what she told me."

"We weren't standing far away and heard."

Nolan shook his head in frustration. "So now all of you know that Mama Laverne's friend's granddaughter is the woman she's picked out for me."

"Yes, and we got a name. Reese and I overheard Mama Laverne tell Aunt Marilyn that your future wife's name is Ivy Chapman."

"Like hell the woman is my future wife." And Nolan couldn't care less about her name. He'd never met her and didn't intend to. "All this time I thought Mama Laverne was plotting to marry the woman's granddaughter off to Lee. She set me up real good."

Corbin didn't say anything and Nolan was glad because for the moment he needed the silence. It didn't matter to him one iota that so far every one of his cousins whose wives had been selected by his great-grandmother were madly in love with their spouses and saw her actions as a blessing and not a curse. What mattered was that she should not have interfered in the process. And what bothered him more than anything was knowing that he was next on her list. He didn't want her to find him a wife. When and if he was ready for marriage, he was certainly capable of finding one on his own.

"You've come up with a plan?" Corbin interrupted Nolan's thoughts to ask.

Nolan thought of the diabolical plan his cousin Lee had put in place to counteract their great-grandmother's shenanigans and guaranteed to outsmart Mama Laverne for sure. However, in the end, Lee's plan had backfired.

"No, why waste my time planning anything? I simply refuse to play the games Mama Laverne is intent on playing. What I'm going to do is ignore her foolishness and enjoy my life as the newest eligible Madaris bachelor."

He could say that since, at thirty-four, he was ten months older than Corbin, who would be next on their great-grandmother's hit list. "By the time I make my rounds, there won't be a single woman living in Houston who won't know I'm not marriage material," Nolan added.

Corbin chuckled. "That sounds like a plan to me."

"Not a plan, just stating my intentions. I refuse

to let Mama Laverne shove a wife that I don't want down my throat just because she thinks she can and that she should."

After ending the call with his brother, Nolan swallowed the last of his beer. Like he'd told Corbin, he didn't have a plan and wouldn't waste time coming up with one. What he intended to do was to have fun; as much fun as any single man could possibly have.

A huge smile touched his lips as he left the balcony. Walking into his condo, he headed for his bedroom. Quickly removing the tux, he changed into a pair of slacks and a pullover sweater. The night was still young and there was no reason for him not to go out and celebrate the holiday.

As he moved toward his front door, he started humming "Jingle Bells." *Let the fun begin.*

# One

_____

*Fifteen months later...*

Nolan clicked off his mobile phone, satisfied with the call he'd just ended with Lee about his cousin's newest hotel, the Grand MD Paris. Construction of the huge mega-structure had begun three weeks ago. Already it was being touted by the media as the hotel of the future, and Nolan would have to agree.

Due to the hotel's intricate design and elaborate formation, the estimated completion time was two years. You couldn't rush grandeur, and by the time the doors opened, the Grand MD Paris would set itself apart as one of the most luxurious hotels in the world.

This would be the third hotel Lee and his business partner, DeAngelo Di Meglio, had built. First there had been the Grand MD Dubai, and after such astounding success with that hotel, the pair had opened the Grand MD Vegas. Since both hotels had been doing extremely well financially, a decision was made to build a third hotel in Paris. The Grand MD Paris would use state-of-the-art technology while maintaining the rich architectural designs Paris was known for.

Slade, the architect in the Madaris family, had designed all three Grand MD hotels. Nolan would have to say that Slade's design of the Paris hotel was nothing short of a masterpiece. Slade had made sure that no Grand MD hotel looked the same and that each had its own unique architecture and appeal. Slade's twin, Blade, was the structural engineer and had spent the last six months in Paris making sure the groundwork was laid before work on the hotel began. There had been surveys that needed to be completed, soil samples to analyze, as well as a tight construction schedule if they were to meet the deadline for a grand opening two years from now. And knowing Lee and DeAngelo like he did, Nolan expected the Grand MD Paris to open its doors on time and to a fanfare of the likes of a presidential inauguration.

After getting a master's graduate degree at MIT, Nolan had begun working for Chenault Electronics at their Chicago office. Chenault Electronics was considered one of the top ten electronics companies in the world. The owner, Nicholas Chenault, was a family friend, had taken Nolan under his wing and had not only been his boss but his mentor, as well.

After working for Chenault for eight years, Nolan had returned to Houston three years ago to start his own company, Madaris Innovations.

Nolan's company would provide all the electronic and technology work for the Grand MD Paris; some would be the first of its kind anywhere. All high-tech and trend changing. It would be Nolan's first project of this caliber and he appreciated Lee and DeAngelo for giving him the opportunity. Lee and his wife, Carly, spent most of their time in Paris now. Since DeAngelo and his wife, Peyton, were expecting their first child four months from now, DeAngelo had decreased his travel schedule somewhat.

Nolan also appreciated Nicholas for agreeing to partner with him on the project. Chenault Electronics would be bringing years of experience and know-how to the table and Nolan welcomed Nicholas's skill and knowledge.

Nolan had enjoyed the two weeks he'd spent in Paris. He would have to go back a number of times this year for more meetings and he looked forward to doing so, since Paris was one of his favorite places to visit. There was a real possibility that he might have to live there while his electronic equipment was scheduled to be installed.

Nolan leaned back in his chair. In a way, he regretted returning to Houston. Before leaving, he had done everything in his power to become the life of every party, and his reputation as Houston's number one playboy had been cemented. In some circles, he'd been pegged as Houston's One-Night Stander. Now that he was back, that role had to be rekindled, but if he was honest with himself, he wasn't looking forward to the nights of mindless, emotionless sex with women whose names he barely remembered. He only hoped that Ivy Chapman, her grandmother and his great-grandmother were getting the message—he had no intentions of settling down anytime soon. At least not in the next twenty-five years or so.

He rubbed a hand down his face, thinking that while he wouldn't admit to it, he was discovering that living the life of a playboy wasn't all that it was cracked up to be. Most of his dates were one-night stands. There were times he would spend a week with the same woman, and occasionally someone would make it a month, but he didn't want to give these women the wrong idea about the possibility of a future together. He was probably going to have to change his phone number due to the number of messages from women wanting a callback. Women expecting a callback. Women he barely remembered from one sexual encounter to the next. Jeez.

Nolan wondered how his cousins Clayton and Blade, the ones who'd been known as die-hard womanizers in the family before they'd settled down to marry, had managed it all. Clayton had had such an active sex life that he'd owned a case of condoms that he'd kept in his closet. Nolan knew that tidbit was more fact than fiction, since he'd seen the case after Clayton had passed it on to Blade when Clayton had gotten married.

Blade hadn't passed the box on to anyone when he'd married. Not only had he used up the case he'd gotten from Clayton, but he'd gone through a case of his own. Somehow Clayton and Blade had not only managed to handle the playboy life, but each claimed they'd enjoyed doing so immensely at the time.

Nolan, on the other hand, was finding the life of a Casanova pretty damn taxing and way too demanding. And it wasn't even deterring Ivy Chapman.

Nolan picked up the envelope on top of the stack on his desk. He knew what it was and who it had come from. He recalled getting the first one six months ago and he had received several more since then. He wondered why Ivy Chapman was still sending him these little personal notes when he refused to acknowledge them. All the notes said the same thing... *Nolan, I would love to meet you. Call me so it can be arranged. Here is my number...*

Nolan didn't give a royal flip what her phone number was, since he had no intentions of calling her, regardless of the fact that his matchmaking great-grandmother fully expected him to do so. He would continue to ignore Miss Chapman and any correspondence she sent him. He refused to give in to his great-grandmother's matchmaking shenanigans.

He tossed the envelope aside and picked up his

cell phone to call his family and let them know he was back. He had slept off jet lag most of yesterday and hadn't talked to anyone other than his cousin Reese and his brother, Corbin. Reese and his wife, Kenna, were expecting their first baby in June and everyone was excited. For years, Reese and Kenna, who'd met in college, had claimed they were nothing but best friends. However, the family had known better and figured one day the couple would reach the same conclusion. Mama Laverne bragged that they were just another one of her success stories.

Nolan ended the call with his parents, stood and walked over to the window to look out. Like most of his relatives, he leased space in the Madaris Building. His electronics company was across the hall from Madaris Explorations, owned by his older cousin Dex.

He loved Houston in March, but it always brought out dicey weather. You had some warm days, but there were days when winter refused to fade into the background while spring tried emerging. He was ready for warmer days and couldn't wait to spend time at the cottage he'd purchased on Tiki Island, a village in Galveston, last year. He'd hired Ron Siskin, a property manager, to handle the leasing of the cottage whenever he wasn't using it. So far it had turned out to be not only a great investment but also a getaway place whenever he needed a break from the demands of his job, life itself and, yes, of

course, the women who were becoming more demanding by the hour.

The buzzer sounded and he walked back over
to his desk. "Yes, Marlene?" Marlene was an older
woman in her sixties who'd worked for him since he
started the company three years ago. A retired ad-
ministrative assistant for an insurance agent, Marlene had decided to come out of retirement when
she'd gotten bored. She was good at what she did
and helped to keep the office running when he was
in or out of it.

"There's a woman here to see you, Mr. Madaris.
She doesn't have an appointment and says it's important."

Nolan frowned, glancing at his watch. It's wasn't
even ten in the morning. Who would show up at
his office without an appointment and at this hour?
There were a number of family members who worked
in the Madaris Building. Obviously, it wasn't one of
them; otherwise Marlene would have said so. "Who
is she?"

"A Miss Ivy Chapman."

He guessed she was tired of sending notes that
went unanswered. Hadn't she heard around town
what a scoundrel he was? The last man any woman
should be interested in? So what was she doing here?

There was only one way to find out. If she needed
to know why he hadn't responded, that he could certainly tell her. She could stop sending him those
notes or else he would take her actions as a form of

harassment. He had no problem telling her in no un-
certain terms that he was not interested in pursuing
an affair with her, regardless of the fact that his great-
grandmother and her grandmother wanted it to be so.

"Send her in, Marlene."

"Yes, Mr. Madaris."

Nolan had eased into his jacket and straightened
his tie before his office door swung open. The first
thing he saw was a huge bouquet of flowers that
was bigger than the person carrying them. Why was
the woman bringing him flowers? Did she honestly
think a huge bouquet of flowers would work when
her cute little notes hadn't?

He couldn't see the woman's face behind the
huge vase of flowers, and without saying a word,
not even so much as a good morning, she plopped
the monstrosity onto his desk with a loud thump. It
was a wonder the vase hadn't cracked. Hell, maybe
it had. He could just imagine water spilling all over
his desk.

Nolan looked from the flowers that were taking
up entirely too much space on his desk to the woman
who'd unceremoniously placed them there. He was
not prepared for the beauty of the soft brown eyes
behind a pair of thick-rimmed glasses or the perfect
roundness of her face and the creamy cocoa coloring
of her complexion. And he couldn't miss the fullness
of her lips that were pursed tight in anger.

"I'm only going to warn you but this once, Nolan
Madaris. Do not send me any more flowers. Doing

so won't change a thing. I've decided to come tell you personally, the same thing I've repeatedly told your great-grandmother and my grandmother. There is no way I'd ever become involved with you. No way. Ever."

Her words shocked him to the point that he could only stand there and stare at her. She crossed her arms over her chest and stared back. "Well?" she asked in a voice filled with annoyance when he continued to stare at her and say nothing. "Do I make myself clear?"

Finding his voice, Nolan said, "You most certainly do. However, there's a problem and I consider it a major one."

Those beautiful eyes were razor-sharp and directed at him. "And just what problem is that?"

Now it was he who turned a cutting gaze on her. "I never sent you any flowers. Today or ever."

*Find out if Nolan Madaris has finally
met his match in
BEST LAID PLANS
by New York Times bestselling author
Brenda Jackson, available March 2018
wherever HQN Books and ebooks are sold.*

*www.Harlequin.com*

# COMING NEXT MONTH FROM

HARLEQUIN *Desire*

## Available April 3, 2018

### #2581 CLAIM ME, COWBOY

*Copper Ridge* • by Maisey Yates

Wanted: fake fiancée for a wealthy rancher to teach his father not to play matchmaker. Benefits: your own suite in a rustic mansion and money to secure your baby's future. Rules: deny all sizzling sexual attraction and don't fall in love!

### #2582 EXPECTING A SCANDAL

*Texas Cattleman's Club: The Impostor* • by Joanne Rock

Wealthy trauma surgeon Vaughn Chambers spends his days saving lives and his nights riding the ranch. But when it comes to healing his own heart, he finds solace only in the arms of Abigail Stewart, who's pregnant with another man's baby...

### #2583 UPSTAIRS DOWNSTAIRS BABY

*Billionaires and Babies* • by Cat Schield

Single mom Claire Robbins knows her boss is expected to marry well. Taking up with the housekeeper is just not done—especially if her past catches up to her. Falling for Linc would be the ultimate scandal. But she's never been good at resisting temptation...

### #2584 THE LOVE CHILD

*Alaskan Oil Barons* • by Catherine Mann

When reclusive billionaire rancher Trystan Mikkelson is thrust into the limelight, he needs a media makeover! Image consultant Isabeau Waters guarantees she can turn him into the face of his family's empire. But one night of passion leads to pregnancy, and it could cost them everything.

### #2585 THE TEXAN'S WEDDING ESCAPE

*Heart of Stone* • by Charlene Sands

Rancher Cooper Stone owes the Abbott family a huge debt...and he's been tasked with stopping Lauren Abbott from marrying the wrong man! But how can Lauren trust her feelings when she learns her time with Cooper is a setup?

### #2586 HIS BEST FRIEND'S SISTER

*First Family of Rodeo* • by Sarah M. Anderson

Family scandal chases expectant mother Renee from New York City to Texas. But when rodeo and oil tycoon Oliver, her brother's best friend, agrees to hide her in his Dallas penthouse, sparks fly. Will her scandal ruin him, too?

---

HDCNM0318

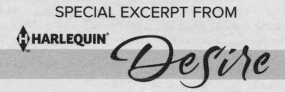
Joshua Grayson looked out the window of his office and did not feel the kind of calm he ought to feel.

He'd moved back to Copper Ridge six months ago from Seattle, happily trading in a man-made, rectangular skyline for the natural curve of the mountains.

But right now he doubted anything would decrease the tension he was feeling from dealing with the fallout of his father's ridiculous ad. Another attempt by the old man to make Joshua live the life his father wanted him to.

The only kind of life his father considered successful: a wife, children.

He couldn't understand why Joshua didn't want the same.

No. That kind of life was for another man, one with another past and another future. It was not for Joshua. And that was why he was going to teach his father a lesson.

He wasn't responsible for the ad in a national paper asking for a wife, till death do them part. But an unsuitable, temporary wife? Yes. That had been his ad.

He was going to win the game. Once and for all. And the woman he hoped would be his trump card was on her way.

The doorbell rang and he stood up behind his desk. She was here. And she was—he checked his watch—late.

A half smile curved his lips.

Perfect.

He took the stairs two at a time. He was impatient to meet his temporary bride. Impatient to get this plan started so it could end.

He strode across the entryway and jerked the door open. And froze.

The woman standing on his porch was small. And young, just as he'd expected, but… She wore no makeup, which made her look like a damned teenager. Her features were fine and pointed; her dark brown hair hung lank beneath a ragged beanie that looked like it was in the process of unraveling while it sat on her head.

He didn't bother to linger over the rest of the details—her threadbare sweater with too-long sleeves, her tragic skinny jeans—because he was stopped, immobilized really, by the tiny bundle in her arms.

A baby.

His prospective bride had come with a baby.

Well, hell.

*Don't miss*
*CLAIM ME, COWBOY*
*by* New York Times *bestselling author Maisey Yates,*
*part of her* **COPPER RIDGE** *series!*

*Available April 2018 wherever*
*Harlequin® Desire books and ebooks are sold.*

www.Harlequin.com

Want to give in to temptation with
steamy tales of irresistible desire?

Check out **Harlequin® Presents®**,
**Harlequin® Desire** and
**Harlequin® Kimani™ Romance** books!

## New books available every month!

---

### CONNECT WITH US AT:

Harlequin.com/Community

 Facebook.com/HarlequinBooks

Twitter.com/HarlequinBooks

Instagram.com/HarlequinBooks

Pinterest.com/HarlequinBooks

ReaderService.com

**ROMANCE WHEN
YOU NEED IT**

PGENRE2017